Head over heels

The wind changed direction, and suddenly the sky was flat as a cookie sheet. Clouds the color of charcoal pressed down close. Rain was close enough that Tres could smell it.

He didn't mind. He didn't have far to go, and besides, he was dizzy with happiness as he rode along the fenceline. Robin Welch liked him, he was working toward getting the prettiest mare in Wooster County, and he was a born roper. Everything seemed possible.

Throw a Hungry Loop

**Dona
Schenker**

Borzoi Sprinters · Alfred A. Knopf
New York

to my hero, my father,
HERBERT ALEXANDER,
with love and gratitude

Throw
a
Hungry
Loop

one

Tres Bomer shook out his rope, snaked out a loop, and sent the rope singing through the air. He watched with satisfaction as it dropped with perfect accuracy over the dummy horns. He shook it off the horns and stepped back. This time he kept his elbow up and threw a horizontal loop, which came in flat as it wrapped around the dummy horns again.

Oh, he was on a roll now. He absolutely couldn't miss, no matter what. Tres took his hat off and brushed the hair from his forehead with the back of his hand. He was sweating, even though it was January and the thinnest layer of ice covered the grass. The only sound was the rhythmic squeaking of the SLAUGHTER CREEK sign at the ranch entrance as it swayed in the wind.

Tres eyed the blue plastic dummy horns. Slowly, they became a cherry-red calf darting across the yard in front of him. The horse was there, too—the snorting, side-stepping one that showed up every morning about this time. The horse pitched its head impatiently, as if to say, "Don't let it get away. What are you waiting for?"

He jumped on the horse and opened the noose of the rope with a few quick jerks. The sun wasn't up yet, but the sky was filled with bright yellow lights, and the space surrounding him on all sides was filled with grandstands packed with cheering, raucous people eating popcorn and cotton candy. Above the crowd he could hear the rodeo announcer: "And Tres Bomer, riding Mariah. He's a thirteen-year-old cowboy who hails from Summit, Texas."

Tres rode to the back of the box, his pigging string in his mouth. He grabbed the saddle horn and kept the reins low. The barrier went down, and the calf took off like a shot, with the horse leaping after it.

He whirled the rope above his head, all the while concentrating on his wrist and keeping his elbow down. When he released the rope with his fingers, it rolled out in front of him with a hiss and a wavelike motion. It landed over the calf's neck with a snap, while Mariah slid to a sudden stop. Tres's foot was already out of the stirrup, and he jumped to the ground.

He ran down the rope, Mariah backing all the while to keep the rope tight. Tres almost lost his black Resistol hat as he reached for the calf's flank, lifted it in the air with his left hand, and pulled the calf down with his right. When he had the calf on the ground, he gathered three legs in tight and made the tie, throwing his hands in the air as he finished.

The crowd came to their feet with a roar.

Suddenly, a voice boomed from the kitchen door. "What in Lord's name are you doing?"

Tres blinked, and the bright lights faded to a soft pink where the sky in the east outlined the hills with morning colors. The screen door slammed, and his granddaddy's big-roweled spurs jingled as he slowly moved down the porch stairs.

"Practicing my throws, same as always." Tres could feel his face color, and his mouth turned up shyly at the corners. He always wanted to laugh when he was embarrassed.

"Well, it don't look that way to me. You're jumpin' around out here like popcorn in a hot skillet. Sometimes I'm pretty sure your think box is addled, boy." His granddaddy loomed on the porch in the drop-seat long-handled underwear that he wore to bed every night. He had pulled on his boots; Tres was pretty sure he never, ever, took those drop-shanked spurs off his boots.

Tres watched him climb the porch stairs. He climbed stiffly and slowly, sliding his big hand along the rail, until his broad shoulders and big silver head and tall body disappeared into the kitchen. Most people looked ridiculous or vulnerable in long underwear, but Granddaddy just looked big and made other people feel ridiculous.

Everyone in Summit called him Senior. It was a proper name for him if you held with names that described the way people looked and acted. Just as Junior was a proper name for Tres's father, that was for sure. Tres, pronounced like "trace," meant three in Spanish, a fact that made him feel glum sometimes. He hoped it wasn't a bad omen, because he never wanted to come in third in anything, except maybe schoolwork.

Well, that would be the end of that because he had no intention of ever naming a future child of his Quatro, or Justice Edward Bomer, which was the true name they all shared.

Tres gathered up the nylon rope and put the roping dummy in the corner of the yard where he'd kept it since Senior had taught him to rope when he was five. His daddy, red-eyed and frowsy-haired, banged out the kitchen door and called the dogs. An old blue tick hound and two yellow Labs appeared from under the porch steps and ambled to a trough, where his father laid out their food and patted them affectionately.

Tres smiled and swung the rope above his head. He pointed his hand downward, dragging the loop forward and swinging it out so that it caught around his father's leg just below the knee as he stepped backward.

"Durned if you ain't got me again." Junior grinned and leaned down to release the rope.

Tres pulled the rope gently so that his father had to skip out to the yard on one foot to keep from falling. His belly hung over his belt like a feed bag, and his shirttail hung out from his jeans jacket, making him look like a sloppy, overgrown adolescent. Everyone said that Tres, with his dark hair and eyes, was the spittin' image of his daddy when he was a boy, before Junior had started drinking and gotten fat.

"When are you going to quit cuttin' the fool and grow up?" Junior said, waggling a finger.

" 'Bout the time you do, Daddy," Tres said.

"Then you ain't never growing up, poor baby." Junior put a big arm around Tres's neck and pulled him in for a bear hug.

Tres didn't mind. His grandmother had died when Junior was a baby, and his own mother had taken off years ago. Tres didn't even remember her. The only female relative Tres knew was his great-aunt Celie in Summit, and she was stronger on passing out gossip than on giving hugs.

"Do me a favor," Junior whispered as they climbed the porch steps.

Tres leaned toward Junior. He knew what was coming.

"Don't irritate your granddaddy this morning. I got me a headache, and I ain't in the mood for a fight." Junior rubbed his eyes.

"I couldn't hear you good. Sorry," Tres teased.

He was determined to talk to his granddaddy again about getting a new horse. Red, Tres's cow pony, had died of old age a couple of months before, and Tres had been desperate for a roping horse ever since.

Junior's mare, Bess, wouldn't let anyone but Junior ride her, and his granddaddy's horse was too high-spirited. The hired hands that drifted in and out used their own horses, because Senior was too frugal to feed and care for animals that weren't used every day.

Tres had tried to make them think he just wanted something to trot around on. His daddy usually tried to get Tres whatever he wanted, but he'd been hoarding his money and seemed tighter than Senior lately. Even if Junior would buy the horse, Tres's granddaddy would put a stop to it. The only way was to convince Senior, maybe make a bargain with him.

His granddaddy had cooked breakfast. The biscuits lying in the tin pan on the table were flat and hard looking, and there was a scorched smell in the air. Three slices of fried ham lay on a greasy platter.

Senior sat at the table, drinking a big mug of black coffee. He scowled at Tres's English paper as if it were full of foreign-language phrases he didn't understand.

"There's a spelling mistake in the first paragraph." He looked Tres full in the face.

"Nobody's perfect, Granddaddy."

" 'Receive' isn't spelled r-e-c-i-e-v-e."

"Well, it's pretty close. It has the same letters."

"Miz West told me at the conference that you memorize spelling words for the test and forget 'em the minute it's over. Says they just fly right out of your head." Senior sank his big teeth into a biscuit, making a crunching noise. "You need to spend less time with that rope and more time with your books. You've got to run the Slaughter Creek someday. Things is changing so fast, it's the educated man that's going to make a go of it."

Oh, boy, thought Tres. I'm in for another "bringing up" lecture. Tres looked over at Junior, who seemed as nervous as a chicken with a coyote. Any hint of an ar-

8

gument in the air sent Junior searching for a way to make things right.

"Boy, these biscuits are sure burned," Junior blurted out. "But dang if I don't love 'em that way," he added quickly, as if he had thought better of it.

Tres's heart was pounding so loud he could hear it in his ears. "Granddaddy, if I was to promise to bring my grades up, could you see clear to getting a roping horse for me?"

Senior's face turned dark and closed.

"Why does it have to be a roping horse? Why not just a plain old riding horse?" He narrowed his eyes, and there was something about the way they had suddenly gone cold that made Tres know he could see right through him.

Tres knew he should just hush up.

"Well, to run a ranch I need to ride and I need to be a good roper, don't I?" Tres asked, sliding past the question.

"Son, when you're running this ranch, they're going to be issuing cowboys Honda motorcycles. Your time would be better spent learning to fly a helicopter. Some of the big ranches are already using them." Senior sat back in his chair, pulled his Bull Durham out, and started rolling a cigarette.

"Oh, shoot. Tres is too young for a motorcycle or a helicopter," Junior said, his face breaking into a whiskery grin.

"Hush! You irritate me," Senior snapped at Junior. He looked from one to the other as a doctor would look at two patients. This one's a hopeless case, the grim set of his mouth said when he looked at Junior, but the other one could pull through.

"I know what's going on here because I see you practice, morning, noon, and night. You aim to be another Phil Lynn or Roy Cooper, a *rodeo* star," Senior said. He cupped his hand around the cigarette to light it, even though there wasn't any wind in the house.

"Maybe," Tres murmured.

His granddaddy had been a rodeo star when he was a few years older than Tres. He'd given it up, just quit one day, and come home to run his family's ranch.

"You think rodeos is all glory and fine clothes and winning money. It ain't true. I wasted four years of my life on the rodeo circuit, and I'm a stove-up old cowboy today because of it. The truth about rodeos ain't the glory or the crowds clapping for you," Senior said.

"Well, what is the truth, Granddaddy?" Tres asked innocently. He'd heard it all before, but he never grew tired of it.

"Misery, son. That's the truth of it. Finding rides in the middle of the night from one rodeo to the next, when you're so tired you could fall asleep standing up. You have to learn to live on one hot dog a day because you never have more than five dollars in your pocket. Why, your body gets as hard and skinny as a jackrabbit that ain't fit to eat. Ten people, sometimes fifteen, sleep in a room, and I never been to a rodeo that stops for cold or rain or mud." Senior drew it all out in the air with his big hands.

Tres nodded, over and over. Excitement welled up inside him like tears. He tried to make his face smooth and blank and patient, so his granddaddy would go on.

Maybe you couldn't hang in there, Granddaddy, he thought, but I could.

"Rodeo life ain't just being able to stick out a bull ride or tie a calf faster than anyone else. It's having your head caved in if you're not lucky or your knees popped out, both your legs broke at the same time, and your lungs punctured by your own ribs. It's a wonder I can walk today.

"The sadness of it is," Senior continued, "that those old boys don't always know when to stop. They just keep trying to jump on the glory train long after they should have settled down, or they turn into bar dogs like your daddy there."

Junior rolled his eyes at Tres. He got up and pulled the leftover glazed ham he'd made for supper the night before from the refrigerator. Cutting a thick slab, he put it between two pieces of homemade bread for Tres's school lunch.

"Daddy's not a bar dog," Tres said, snapping back to reality. "He never was on the rodeo circuit, neither."

"Nuff said," Senior replied. He scraped his chair back and grabbed his hat off the rack and went out the kitchen door. The jeep's engine fired, and Tres knew that Senior was off to check his registered longhorns. He rode his horse only when he had to now, because his rheumatism was so bad.

Tres watched his father's back as Junior packed his

lunch, and he felt miserable. If he hadn't asked for a horse, Granddaddy might not have called Junior a bar dog. There was some truth to it, and everyone knew it, but he was a lot of other things, too. He was the best cook in Summit, and his granddaddy almost never had to call a vet, because Junior had an uncanny knack for being able to treat animals.

"I'm sorry about irritating Granddaddy. He gets mad at me and takes it out on you," Tres said.

"You're not kidding." There was a bitter tone in Junior's voice that Tres hadn't heard before. "Anyway"—he brightened—"I'm putting a fortune cookie in your lunch bag. They sell 'em at the grocery store in Summit now."

Tres wrapped a piece of last night's corn bread in a paper napkin.

"You better get a move on. You may have missed the school bus already." Junior looked at his watch.

"Tack and Coot are picking me up," Tres said.

"You tell Tack to watch his speedometer."

Tres knew that Junior felt sorry for him about the horse and would try to cheer him up.

"Hey, Tres," he called as Tres walked down the road to the highway. "Get off the bus at the Taylors' place after school. I've got to deliver some oats, and I'll fetch you there."

Tres nodded and kept walking. Wasn't that just like Junior, to think a visit to a horse ranch would cheer him up? Going to Coot Taylor's ranch was like going to a candy store without any money.

The little white-faced Hereford cow was waiting for

him in the usual spot behind the barbed-wired fence at the end of the road. She was round as a little barrel now and already making a milk bag. Granddaddy had taken her mother in a trade, and she was the only cow left on the place that wasn't a longhorn.

He gave her the corn bread and pulled some sticker burs from her muzzle as she ate it. The heifer was an accident waiting to happen. There always seemed to be a tin can stuck on her front foot or cactus thorns embedded in her tongue so that she couldn't eat. Senior, and even Junior, had decided long ago that she was a pest, but Tres cared for her as if she were a troublesome pet. In return she'd been good-natured when he and Red had chased her across the pasture, trying out new throws and stops.

The memory of those days rose up in his mind as clear as a photograph. What a fairy tale it all seemed now. They'd been a team, but Red was dead, and the heifer was pregnant and too big to chase.

He fished the fortune cookie out of his lunch bag. He crunched on the hard cookie and swallowed, trying to push down the lump in his throat. The little slip of white paper inside read: "Confucius say, Amazing things occur today."

He crumpled it in his hand and shoved it into the pocket of his jeans. It wasn't until much later that he remembered the fortune, and wondered how the man who wrote those sayings could have known.

two

Ten minutes before the final bell was supposed to ring, a red Buick convertible made a loud rubber-stinking stop beside Tres. The heifer, udders flopping, ran across the pasture.

Tres got in beside Coot and glanced at his brother, Tack, behind the wheel. "I don't mean to complain, Tack, but me and Coot have enough tardy slips to paper the side of a barn."

"Lighten up for once, huh, Tres?" Tack immediately grabbed a shoe box from the back seat and took a horny toad out of it. He reached around outside and put the lizard on the windshield in front of him.

"What's that?" Tres asked.

"Protection," Tack said. "Ticket protection." The car shot onto the road, spitting gravel in every direction. The lizard hung on as they sped down the highway toward Summit.

Tres's mind was reeling. Coot, his red hair flying in the cold wind, grinned like a banshee. Tres had seen it happen a hundred times. Tack would come up with some cuckoo scheme that could get them all in trouble. "Watch this," they'd both say, the way other people would say: "Oh, boy, we're going to get out the poles and go fishing!" Happy, looking forward to it.

Tres couldn't keep his eyes off the poor lizard. Its little toes were plastered against the windshield, and its eyes were bugged. Tres tried to ask Coot why it was there, but the cold wind whipped his words away.

On the outskirts of Summit, Tack shot by a highway patrolman. The patrol car turned on its lights and siren and chased Tack to the Summit City Limits sign.

"Where's the fire, son?" the patrolman said, coming to the window.

"Ain't no fire, sir. It's this dang horny toad crawled on my windshield and scared me to death. I sped up, like anybody would, trying to knock it off. Didn't want it to bite these here boys," Tack said earnestly.

The patrolman wrinkled his eyebrows. "Funny time of year for horny toads. It ain't even spring yet."

"Guess it's the sun being out that's got 'em crawlin'," Tack said.

"Good recovery," Coot whispered to Tres.

"Well, I'm givin' you a warning this time, son, but if a critter crawls up there again, stop the car and take it off. Hear?"

"That's just what I aim to do, Officer." Tack jumped

out of the car and took the lizard off the windshield and put it back in the shoe box.

"My little brother and his buddy here can take it to school for show-and-tell," Tack said, staring at Coot as if this were the beginning of a long, serious lecture. "Now, you let it go when the kids have seen it. Keepin' a horny toad is as bad as shootin' a mockingbird."

Coot groaned and pulled his hat down over his eyes. Tres felt the corners of his mouth twitch upward while Tack waved and yessirred at the patrolman.

The patrolman shook his head and walked back to his car. When he drove off, Coot and Tack had a fit of hissing laughter.

TRES hated handing the tardy slip to Mr. Turner, who despised him. Last year Turner had sent a note home complaining of Tres's short attention span. Senior had lectured him about it and sent a note back saying Turner had weak brain waves. To make matters worse, Tres had Turner for math *and* Spanish this year.

Turner looked at Tres from behind his glasses with hard little BB-shot eyes.

"You were *detained,* Mr. Bomer?"

"That's right, sir."

"By *whom* were you detained, Mr. Bomer?"

"Oh, the highway patrol stopped us . . . ," Tres began to explain.

"Really?" Mr. Turner appeared fascinated. "Why does that not surprise me?"

The class laughed. It sounded far away. Tres was more

aware of the faint buzzing in his ears. I've been here thirty seconds, he thought, and I already look like a fool.

Coot sidled past Tres and took a seat behind Delia Rivers, a fat girl. He lowered himself in his seat until nothing of him showed.

"May I sit down now?" Tres asked.

"Oh, by all *means*. My day is not complete without *you* here."

Tres gave a little nervous laugh—he was the only one who laughed—and sat down.

Turner turned to write a math problem on the board. Coot took the opportunity to pass Tres a piece of paper that had been folded and unfolded so many times it looked like an old treasure map. It was a racing cover, or had been, featuring quarter horses.

Mr. Turner gave a loud, heartrending sigh. "Mr. Bomer, *please*. I get so upset when I don't have the attention of all my *scholars*," he said sarcastically.

The class twittered, all except Coot and Bubba Wayne.

"Yes, sir," Tres said.

Turner cracked his knuckles one by one. After the last knuckle, he said, "Since you have failed to turn the burning flame of your curiosity to the blackboard, you can spend lunch in detention hall."

THAT afternoon was bright and cold, the kind of weather Tres hated when he was feeling glum and put upon. The sun streamed down through fat white clouds on the kids as they poured out of Summit Junior School, chattering and blinking in the sunshine.

Tres climbed on the bus, nodded at Mr. Peavy, the driver, and went to the back, where no one else liked to sit.

Placing his black Resistol low on his forehead, he closed his eyes to sort things out. Granddaddy had him over a barrel. He hadn't said he wouldn't buy a new horse for Tres; he just hadn't said he would. There was no question of working for the money, either. All the chores he did at Slaughter Creek were expected and done for free.

Lord, he had to have a horse to practice with. It had been two months since Red died, and Red had been so old it was hard to practice with him, anyway.

It was bad enough that he couldn't compete in any of the junior rodeos because his granddaddy thought it was a waste of time and money. If he only had a decent horse, he could practice on his own. When he was old enough to go out on the rodeo circuit, he'd be the best roper around.

It looked bleak, all right, he thought, peering out from under the brim of his hat. The bus was almost full now. Tres saw Coot standing in front. He was scanning the crowd. Tres knew he should motion him back, but he didn't feel like talking.

Someone pulled Coot into a seat up front, before Tres could decide what to do. Mr. Peavy shut the bus doors, told everyone to "listen up," and began his usual lecture about bus manners.

Tres tuned him out as Robin Welch, a ninth grader, came down the aisle. He felt his heart lurch. She struggled with a heavy stack of books and searched for a place to sit. The only place left was next to Tres, and as he stood up to let her in, her gleaming black hair brushed his face.

The bus pulled onto the highway, and Tres watched Robin, entranced. She pulled one of her wool gloves off with her teeth as she stared out the window. Her skin was the color of apricots. There were little gold hoops in her ears, and her hair fell perfectly straight to her shoulders.

"What are you staring at?" She turned and looked at him with deep-blue eyes.

Tres faced forward and felt his face color. In spite of himself, he grinned.

"You." He cleared his throat. "You just moved here, right?"

"Yes. We came from Austin last month," she said, as if answering a dumb question.

So Robin Welch is snotty, Tres thought. No problem. Tres had a theory that most snotty girls were just shy, even if they were pretty. He had no earthly idea where this theory came from, never having been shy himself.

The silence lengthened.

"You're an eighth grader, aren't you?" she finally asked.

"Well, not really. I was held back in kindergarten," Tres lied. He looked at her again. She was twirling her shoe on the toe of her foot, and Tres saw she was wearing red socks. He couldn't believe how lucky he was to be sitting next to her.

"That's not something to be proud of." She glanced at him and lifted an eyebrow.

"I wasn't dumb or anything. I was just a nasty little kid. I went through this stage when I spit on people in the lunchroom, and I shoved in line a lot, too."

"Really? I always wanted to do that." Robin turned toward him in her seat. Her dark, shining hair fell into her eyes.

She's interested now, he thought.

"Oh, yeah. I used to beat Coot Taylor black and blue at the sandpile every day. He lost most of his baby teeth because of me."

"This is terrible." Her own white teeth showed in a smile.

"The clincher came when I held Bubba Wayne down while the teacher was in the bathroom. I made him eat a whole jar of paste. It affected his speech. He stuttered until last year," Tres said earnestly.

"Is this true?" she asked, narrowing her brows.

"Nah. I wouldn't do stuff like that," Tres said.

Robin laughed so hard she started to cough. Tres wondered how it was possible to feel so good all of a sudden. They rode in silence for a while.

"Why don't you visit us at Slaughter Creek? I mean, you live just down the road. I could meet you halfway," he offered.

"How do you know where I live?" She was still smiling a tiny bit.

"Well, you know how it is." Of all the dumb things to say, he thought.

Actually, everyone knew who Robin Welch was and where she lived. She was new and pretty, and her father had bought the old Draco ranch and put a swimming pool in the backyard.

"Summit is full of cowboys, and I'm not sure I like them," she said, looking him up and down. "You're definitely a cowboy."

The bus was slowing down. They were in front of Coot's place.

"Yeah, but that's okay. I'll be the cowboy, and you can be the Indian," Tres said.

"You're a big flirt for an eighth grader."

Tres stood up and grabbed his book bag. "My great-aunt Celie says all Bomer men are born flirts. It's sure gotten my daddy in a heap of messes."

"I'll bet," Robin said.

"Well, see you around." Tres stood staring at Robin until Coot grabbed his arm and pulled him off the bus.

Tres felt dazed. They passed the tall sign with a white horse on top and the words TAYLOR HORSE RANCH below. Tres looked back to the highway. The yellow bus was just a spot in the distance. Suddenly, he was aware of Coot standing in the road, staring at him.

"Why didn't you wait for me like you usually do? You mad at me about lunch detention?" Coot asked.

"Nah. I was in such a bad mood I forgot."

"You don't look like you're in any bad mood now," Coot said.

"I'm not!" Tres answered. "Well, see, I was upset about not having a horse."

"Aha!" said Coot. "And someone gave you one on the bus?"

"No, course not. I sat next to Robin Welch, and she cheered me up. We got along great."

"What's your biggest dream?" Coot asked, changing the subject. There was an excited look in his eyes.

"Winning silver trophy buckles as big as cake plates. You know that," Tres said. He looked back. The yellow bus had disappeared. He felt the need to whine. "I gotta have a horse."

"Who's your best friend?" Coot grabbed him suddenly, which made Coot appear a little nuts.

"You are, stupid," Tres answered.

"Well, I've been trying to tell you all day. I wanted to this morning, but the horny toad . . . I'm sorry for gettin' you in trouble with Turner, by the way, but anyway, now I'll just show you." Coot was rattling on like a baboon, as if Tres might disappear if he slowed down.

What on earth? wondered Tres.

They passed the white metal gates that surrounded Coot's house, and took a shortcut through the horse barn, where the sweet scent of hay and sweaty leather was in the air. Foals paced and thrust their muzzles through the bars on the stall doors. The stalls were spacious and filled with clean hay.

Mr. and Mrs. Taylor sat in an office at the end of the stable, talking on two different phones. A small space heater was going full blast, and there were photographs of prize-winning racehorses on the walls. Mrs. Taylor hung up the phone and came to the door with a plate of sugar cookies.

"Sweeties." She beamed at them. Mrs. Taylor was the kind of mother who loved having kids around.

"No time for chitchat, Mom," Coot said. He grabbed the plate of cookies and headed outside, where a quarter horse, black and shiny as a crow's wing, was walking circles on the hot walker. There were pastures divided into large squares by white metal fences as far as the eye could see. Tres knew that most of these horses were headed for the racetracks at Del Rio and Ruidosa.

It was a beautiful world, different from Slaughter Creek. There, the acres were grazed by the quick-tempered, unpredictable longhorns that his granddaddy sold to other ranchers.

Coot led him to a small indoor arena, where the Taylors had their horse sales. They sat astride a gate and watched Tack ride a sleek chestnut mare. She was clean-limbed, with high withers and long sloping shoulders, and her coat was so smooth it shone like silk. When Tack stopped her to adjust his spurs, Tres could see that she was nervous, and she danced from side to side.

It was the second time that day that Tres's heart flopped like a catfish out of water. She looked like Mariah, the quarter horse he daydreamed about every morning, except that she had a white blaze and three quarter-stockinged feet.

"Coot boy! Where did she come from?" Tres asked.

"Tack brought her in from the racetrack at Eagle Pass last night. He bought her cheap because she was supposed to run Triple A time. She had some trouble in the starting gates and only ran Double A." Tres hadn't seen Coot this excited since he was chosen for hall monitor in fifth grade.

Tack had the mare in a gallop now. Tres could see he was trying to teach her to stop, but instead of letting her gather her feet up each time, Tack jerked the reins back so hard that she pitched her head and balked.

"Why's he tearing her head off like that? He doesn't need to use that ring bit, either. It's too severe." Tres couldn't stand to see any animal mistreated, but this horse was something special.

"He's trying to teach her to stop fast. He has a notion that he can make her into a cutting horse, thinks he can get more money for her that way. But you know Tack." Coot shrugged his shoulders, and sharpened his pocketknife on his boot heel.

Tres didn't need an explanation. Tack knew about racehorses, but racehorses knew nothing but straight. He didn't know from sic 'em about training a cutting or a roping horse. Even if he did, he couldn't do it because he had the patience of a jackrabbit and a hair-trigger temper.

"It's a pure shame, Coot. The best place for that horse is behind a cow, slow and easy. He'll ruin her." Tres watched Tack dig his spurs into the mare's side. He pulled on the reins, and the mare balked. He tried again, jerking the mare's head and slapping the reins hard against her neck.

The mare lowered her neck, then rose up on her hind

feet. She whirled around in a complete circle and dumped Tack on the ground.

Tres laughed, trying hard not to let it show. This is one great horse, he thought, and his spirits soared.

Tack's face was red and sweat-streaked, and his eyes were a chilly blue. He grabbed the reins and got back on the horse.

"He can't ruin her if you buy her," Coot said.

three

W here would I get the money for a horse like that?" Tres asked.

"When she has her calf, that purebred heifer of yours should bring a bundle," Coot said. "You could sell the heifer and calf and have plenty left over to buy the horse."

"She ain't really my cow, and you know it. Grand-daddy just gave her to me to raise," Tres said.

"She should be yours," Coot said fiercely. "You fed her with a bottle when her mama died, and you halter-broke her. You nursed her through that bad case of pinkeye last winter. You stitched her up when she got caught in barbed wire and her wounds festered last summer. She'd be dead three times if it weren't for you."

"What should be and what is are two different things, Coot." But he was thinking; he was thinking as hard as he had ever thought.

"There's just no telling what kind of messes that heifer's going to get into now that she's pregnant." Coot's face flushed a little redder than usual. "She's been more trouble than she's worth since the day she was born. It's a wonder the old so-and-so hasn't given her to you already."

He had never thought about it before, but he knew immediately that Coot was right. Tres had a strange light feeling in his chest. It might work, he told himself. If I bring it up in just the right way, it might work.

Tack rode over on the mare, a grin on his dark face. "I'm a genius, right?"

"She's a great horse, Tack." Tres watched Tack take a tin of Skoal from his pocket and place a pinch inside his lower lip.

"No, I mean the horny toad trick. Genius, right?"

"Right." Tres ran his hand along the mare's muzzle and rubbed her neck. What he liked best was the look in her eyes: they were bright and gentle but very alert. Her coat glistened from good feed and care, but Tres saw where Tack had left spur marks on her side.

"Tres wants to buy the mare, Tack. Problem is, he has to wait until his registered heifer has her calf to sell her. If you could hold on to her for him, you wouldn't have to worry with training her. He could do that," Coot offered.

Tack spread his hands. "I'd like to help you out, Tres, you being a family friend and all. The problem is, I've got a gambling debt to take care of. The first man that puts twelve hundred dollars in my pocket walks away with her."

Tres felt himself about to panic. "Then let me take her to Slaughter Creek and train her for you there. It's something I know a lot about. Besides, you're busy with more important stuff." His heart beat wildly, and he hated the wheedling tone in his voice.

Tack's mouth cracked into a smile. "No offense, Tres, but tight as Senior is, you think he's going to feed and board an extra animal? Not to mention let you take time off from your chores to train her."

As Tres watched him turn the mare and walk her slowly out of the ring, he knew that Tack was right.

By the time Junior came to pick him up, jumbled emotions made Tres feel queasy.

"Ain't you got anything to say this evening?" Junior drove down the highway with one hand on the steering wheel.

Tres wanted to spill everything—but no, he had to handle this situation carefully.

"Tack has a horse I could learn to like, Daddy," Tres said, trying to be blasé.

"How much?" Junior asked.

Tres cleared his throat. "Twelve hundred dollars."

"Whoo-ee! I guess mebbe I could like that horse, too."

Tres watched Junior's face until the realization hit it.

"Wait a minute, honey," Junior said. "You ain't aiming to bring this up at suppertime? Twice in one day? Just tell me now, 'cause I'm headin' straight to the Midnight Rodeo if you are."

You'll end up there sometime tonight anyway, Tres

thought. He felt a jolt of anger. I need your help, Daddy, but if I ask for it you'll wind up at the bar two hours ahead of schedule.

He glanced nervously at Junior. Tres had gotten him all worried and upset.

"Nah. Just making conversation," Tres said. "Don't worry about it none." He reached out and patted Junior's arm. He looked as if he needed it.

TRES knew he'd have to deal with his grand-daddy head-on. He spent the next week watching him like a hawk. He wanted to find just the right time to ask about the heifer. But Granddaddy was touchy as a teased snake, same as always, and Tres walked wide around him.

Coot called Sunday night. "What did the old man say?"

"I ain't asked him yet." Tres doubted if anyone in Texas felt as miserable as he did. He'd lost weight, and his eyes felt scratchy from lack of sleep.

"Aw, man. Tack's had two buyers out this weekend."

"Is she gone?" Tres's heart lurched.

"Naw, they was just tire kickers," Coot said.

"Hoo-boy. Two weeks ago I'd have sworn anything with wool, hide, or hair would do. Now I can't think about anything but that mare."

"Quit thinkin' so much and talk to him about it," Coot urged. "You're only askin' for the heifer, remember?"

"He's very liable to say no, Coot. What am I going to do then?"

Monday afternoon he felt sullen and sluggish as mud.

He put his head down on his desk in Spanish class. His mind was full of disturbing questions. What if Granddaddy wouldn't give him the heifer? What if Tack sold the mare before he had a chance to buy her?

Tack had a mean streak. What if he ruined the mare in the meantime? Everybody knew that whether a horse turned out to be a good roping horse or a lousy one depended on the trainer.

He could hear Glenda Ray and Debbie Barnes laughing softly beside him.

"This class smells like a locker room," Debbie said.

"That's because Tres Bomer has BO." Glenda giggled.

Tres knew they wanted a response, but their voices sounded as if they were down a well. He was startled awake just in time to see Mr. Turner hurl a piece of chalk with such velocity that it shattered against the back wall.

The class laughed as Tres sat there blinking.

"In the hall, Bomer." Mr. Turner waited for Tres and stalked out behind him.

Turner peered at Tres coldly through his rimless glasses. "Are you intent on making a fool out of me?"

"No, *sir*. I thought you were trying to make a fool out of me."

"I do not show up late to teach you, carry on conversations while you talk, and sleep in your presence." Mr. Turner pulled himself up to his full height.

"Well, sir. You've sure got a point there. I've got a terrible problem, and it's sapping my energy," Tres whined.

"Solve it."

"Sir?"

"I said, 'Solve it,' Bomer," Turner thundered.

He put his hand on the doorknob.

"Wait a minute, Mr. Turner. It ain't that easy of a problem."

"Here is Turner's Law: It wouldn't be a problem if it didn't have a solution. It is true in math, and it is true in life."

"Yeah, but what if you want something that's almost impossible to get?"

"Here is Turner's Second Law: It's easier to get what you want than to feel bad about not having it."

Tres felt strangely relieved. This was logical. "You know, Mr. Turner, I've been wanting to tell you that I'm really not so bad. You're not so bad, neither."

"Okay, you've brought me close to tears," Turner said, and walked back into class.

Tres got off the school bus an hour later, knowing that something had to be done. It would be better to have a flat no from Granddaddy than to go on in limbo.

You're goin' to *quit* being such a scaredy-cat, and I mean *right this minute,* he told himself. He squared his shoulders and squeezed up all the courage he had. Walking down the road from the highway to the house, he rehearsed all his arguments.

Senior and Junior stood in a small corral behind the barn, looking toward a thicket. Tres couldn't see anything there, but Senior was laughing so hard that he held his belly and gasped for air.

A good sign, Tres told himself. He discarded the speech he'd planned and plunged right in.

"Granddaddy, I've found me the perfect horse. It's over at Taylor's ranch. Now, the way I figure it, that pregnant heifer would never have made it this far if it wasn't for me. If you was to give her to me, I could sell her when the calf comes and have enough to buy the mare." Tres was out of breath.

Senior's face took on a puzzled expression for a moment. He cupped his hand to his ear and asked Tres to repeat himself. Senior had heard, but he just wanted time to think, Tres realized. His initial courage failed a little, but he repeated his speech anyway.

"By granny, ain't he gettin' highfalutin'?" Senior asked Junior when Tres finished.

Junior stared at the ground. "You know he's right," he muttered.

Tres could have kissed his daddy. He knew how hard it was for him to take sides in any discussion.

"Well, now, I was aiming to sell that heifer myself when she has her calf next month," Senior said, scratching his jaw. "She's been a heap of trouble, but she's a valuable animal, all right."

Tres heard a sudden loud popping in the thicket. A shaggy-looking animal crashed out of the brush and came up to the corral fence. At first, Tres thought it was a deformed horse. It sat back on its haunches, tucked in its front feet, and fired itself over the fence, landing three feet from Tres.

"What's that?" Tres asked, stepping back.

"That's ol' Sissy Belle." Senior was grinning like a shoat in hog heaven. "We had her in the corral, but she liked the looks of that thicket yonder and jumped right over."

Tres had seen only a handful of mules in his life, but he knew that this one was a particularly pitiful specimen. Her ratty coat was the color of a gopher, and it was rough and unkempt. She was so hogbacked that her spine curved upward in the middle. Her knees were knocked and her hooves were splayed, and the ribs showing through her hide reminded Tres of fish bones after a trout fry.

"What's she doing here?" Tres asked.

"Miz Gertrude sweet-talked your daddy here into taking her. Seems she's moved to Dallas. Sissy Belle looks like she belongs in a pet food can to me, but your daddy thinks she can still be of some use." He let out another loud hoot of laughter.

Junior's neck colored, but he kept a good-natured look on his face. Tres knew he got fed up with being the butt of every joke, but he never showed it. He felt a sharp pang of love and pity for his father, and he forgot about the cow and Mariah.

"Well, maybe she can work. Mules are supposed to be good workers. She looks like she's got some life left in her." Tres couldn't believe his own ears as he heard himself speak.

Sissy Belle came up behind Tres and blew her warm breath down his neck.

"For a wonder, Tres, I can see you and that ol' mule are sweet on each other," Senior said, with a smile that made Tres uneasy.

"Tell you what," he continued. "I got me an idea. You and ol' Sissy Belle ride fence for me in the afternoons after school and run errands to town for me when I need things. When that troublemaking heifer makes it to motherhood, I'll give her to you then, free and clear, and you can buy the horse if you want," Senior said.

"No, sir! What if she can't be ridden? Not to mention what a fool I'll make of myself in town on that old plug. No offense, Daddy," Tres added.

Junior held up his hands. "That's okay."

"I'll admit there ain't no prestige in being mounted on a mule. But that's my offer, take it or leave it. The flames of hell will be as cold as an icicle before I change my mind."

Tres turned to Junior.

"Daddy, this is mean, plain and simple. You know it." He wanted to say that Junior was as much a kid as he was, that he should act like a father, but he couldn't say it. He couldn't say anything. His tongue choked him.

"Tres . . . ," Junior started.

"It ain't mean. It's called working. No sense trying to bullyrag me, boy," Senior said, his big jaw thrust forward. He walked, ramrod straight, back to the house.

Tres looked at the mule. Now, he thought, *here* is trouble. She had to be at least forty years old. It was a wonder she was still alive. He felt stunned. If all his hopes and dreams were tied up in this mangy animal, they were just so much sawdust. A lump rose in his throat. He tried to stifle his tears, but they burned his cheeks.

"Damn! Why do I let him do that?" Junior slapped his hat on his knee. "I always let him win. I'm weak."

"Don't you start that, Daddy. Don't you dare try to make me feel sorry for you," Tres yelled. The tears were bitter on his tongue.

"You gotta help me figure this out," Tres continued. "Nothin's more important to me than getting that mare."

"I didn't mean to get you into this. Gertrude needed help. Oh, son, there's a world of trouble when women enter the picture," Junior glumly philosophized. "Life moves along smoothly, then you discover girls. Between that time and death, it's just one thing after another."

Tres ignored him. "Granddaddy wouldn't have made the offer if he'd thought I'd take him up on it. If there's a way on earth to get that horse, I'm going to do it."

He fastened a rope around Sissy Belle's neck and led her into the barn. He took a bridle from a nail in the harness room and found the saddle that had been Red's. She crab-stepped a little when he put the saddle on her, jerked her head and snorted when he tightened the girth, but that was all. She didn't seem to mind when he slipped a curb bit into her mouth. Tres took it as a good sign. She may not have been ridden in years, but someone had ridden her at some time.

He put his foot in the stirrup and swung up. The saddle shifted forward over her withers. At this rate, he'd be kicking her in the elbows.

35

"She needs to be breeched," Junior said from the barn door. He brought out a leather strap from the tack room, which he fitted across her rump and attached to the saddle. The saddle shifted back, but Tres still felt as if he were sitting on top of a seesaw.

He kicked her to get her going. She took a few stiff-legged steps and stopped. He kicked her again, but she stood firm, making a rattling noise in her nose. He kicked her a few more times. She didn't budge.

"She's showing the whites of her eyes, son," Junior said, backing off.

Tres concluded that the mule wasn't going anywhere, and he gagged on the thought.

"Daddy, hand me that switch yonder," he said.

Junior handed him a mesquite switch and backed off further.

"Now fish or cut bait," Tres commanded, and he gave Sissy Belle a sharp pop on her rump. The mule joggled forward in an unsteady trot, a harsh rattle in her throat. She picked up a little speed as he steered her onto the road.

"Yah-hoo!" Tres yelled, waving his hat at Junior. "She ain't Trigger, but she'll go."

They took a deer trail through a deep mesquite thicket, Sissy Belle's gotched ears flopping back and forth. They came out on the other side of an open pasture, where the grass was dry and gray-brown from the winter. The sharp smell of scrub cedar was in the air. A deer ran across the pasture ahead, its white flag up. It was the time of day that Tres loved best.

He found most of the herd milling around the creek. The old cows looked at him with stupid, hungry eyes and blew their nostrils. Some of them were shadowed by little stiff-legged calves. Rangy brindle steers slurped water and bumped against each other's flanks. Tres topped a rise and found the bull standing by himself, chewing prairie grass slowly, his eyes shut.

He estimated how many sacks of feed they'd need to bring later in the pickup.

He went back and checked the brands and looked at the cattle for signs of lump jaw or cancer eye. When he was satisfied, he rode downstream.

The sun was down low, orange above the dark hills in the west, when they found the heifer. She was nibbling new grass in a stand of box elders, looking placid as you please.

Tres lit down from Sissy Belle, caught the reins in a bush, and approached the heifer slowly. He looked her over. She appeared to have gained close to a hundred pounds, and her red coat was sleek and shiny. He pulled the lower lid of her eye down and saw that it was whitish pink, a good sign.

Whatever problems the heifer had in the past were gone for now. He looked at ol' Sissy Belle, already dozing on three legs. She was a reminder that life was full of sticker burs. He had a team again, though: a shad-bellied mule, a mischief-making heifer, and himself, Tres Bomer.

four

It was thick dark, and the sky was still pin-pricked with stars, when from all sides there rose, like a ship in trouble, a brassy bray. It went on and on, the volume rising and falling.

Tres woke abruptly and groped for his clock. Junior appeared, stumbling around the doorframe, holding his head. He was shaky, and his eyes were bloodshot and bleary from the night before.

"Five-thirty, Daddy. You can set your watch by her. This is the fourth day in a row," Tres said.

"I thought mebbe she'd give us a break, seeing as how it's Saturday." Junior sat down on the end of Tres's bed and buried his head between his hands. "Lord, my poor head can't take it."

Tres raised the window. A blast of cold air hit him in the face.

"Shut up, you jarhead, or I'll blow you to mule heaven!"

Sissy Belle answered with another series of asthmatic brays, which sent Junior to the bathroom to gulp aspirin.

"She ain't goin' to stop her conniptions with you yelling threats at her. There's nothin' for it but to get up," Senior said on his way to the bathroom.

That's fine for him, Tres thought. His granddaddy hadn't been able to sleep much in years anyway.

If Sissy Belle kept to the pattern of the last three days, Tres knew she'd bray on and off like this until the sky lightened in the east. He hadn't minded the first couple of days, because he'd thought that getting up earlier would give him more time to practice his throws. But Sissy Belle's caterwauling across the fence had so unnerved him that he'd gotten a rope burn and a couple of blood blisters. Now he had to practice with a bandanna tied around his hand, and his timing was off.

By the time Tres had dressed, the bitter smell of coffee was in the air. He could hear pans clattering and was relieved to see that his daddy, his face still a little puffy from sleep, was in the kitchen, his hands stuck in a dough of raw eggs and flour. Junior pulled off pieces the size of a golf ball, dipped each end in melted butter, and put them on a greased pan. He sprinkled flour on top of each one and shoved the bake pan in the oven.

He handed Tres a cup of hot coffee. Tres sat at the table and breathed in the steam from the cup. He was always amazed to see his daddy work in the kitchen. Junior was slow and clumsy everywhere else, but in the kitchen he was fast and efficient.

39

Junior broke several eggs into a frying pan and cut off pieces of a German sausage into the pan with them. Watching his father cook made Tres so hungry that his stomach felt as if it were full of thorns. He knew that all this food was Junior's morning-after cure. Starve a fever, feed a hangover.

When the eggs were done, Junior pulled the piping-hot biscuits from the oven and set them before Tres. He spooned the scrambled eggs and sausage out of the frying pan onto Tres's plate. Setting a big bowl of peach preserves on the table, he sat down to serve himself.

The eggs were perfect—hot and fluffy. By the time he'd put away three biscuits and a couple of glasses of orange juice, Tres was looking forward to the day. No school, plenty of time to practice his throws, and maybe a visit to the Taylors' ranch to see Mariah. He could ride fence on Sissy Belle late in the afternoon and check the herd for Granddaddy.

"Tres, I've got a money order for Mr. Tolbert at the hardware store in town. You and Sissy Belle can run it in this morning." Senior loomed in the doorway.

What Tres thought was: Saturday morning, everybody and his dog going into Summit on errands, me on a half-dead mule. Oh, Lord, life is cruel.

"Heck, I can run that money order to Tolbert in the pickup this morning," Junior said, scratching his stomach happily.

Tres blew a sigh of relief.

"If that don't sum up every single thing wrong in this house. I try to give the boy some responsibility, Junior, and you try to jerk it right back. You and me are goin' to oil the blades on that windmill this morning," Senior said, scowling at Junior.

Tres looked at his daddy. Junior picked at his food.

"Granddaddy, I'll walk the money order in. It'll be good exercise," Tres said, a hopeful look on his face.

Senior straightened his broad shoulders and went into his lecture mode.

"No sense walking three miles when you have a perfectly good mount. You need to learn that there ain't no shame in riding a mule any more than there's glory in riding a fancy horse. We struck a bargain. You can send me off to sell hot tamales in hell before I change my mind, boy," Senior said with finality.

Tres decided to get an early start in hopes that he'd beat the crowd into town. He threw the saddle on Sissy Belle and tightened the girth a little harder than he needed to. Her bug eyes shifted from side to side.

Tres felt a sharp pang of anger as he swung into the saddle. "You're so ugly, Sissy Belle, you'd have to sneak up on the trough to get a drink of water."

He popped her on the rump, and they joggled down the gravel road to the two-lane blacktop. It was farm-to-market Road 42, and everyone on the way to Summit traveled it.

He jammed his hat down as far as he could on his head and stayed close to the fence in the brush. Sissy Belle's head pumped rhythmically up and down in front of him. She was breathing in snorts, like an old sow.

Tres tried to get her into a trot but decided she'd need tin cans tied to her tail before she'd speed up today.

"All that braying just wore you out, huh? Well, you can't make a silk purse out of a sow's ear," he said.

An occasional car or diesel truck sped by, but traffic was thin. By the time he saw the steeple of the First Baptist Church on the south edge of Summit, Tres was counting his lucky stars that no one had called to him from the road or even honked at him.

He took a deserted road winding south, even though it would have been shorter to turn east and go straight through town. The road ran into the railroad tracks, and he followed them for a mile until he came to the north end of Main Street.

Tres snuck Sissy Belle up a wide alley behind the hardware store. On the other side of the alley were the backyards of Sheriff Barnes and Mr. Tolbert. Mr. Tolbert's yard was surrounded by a white picket fence to protect Mrs. Tolbert's garden. Sheriff Barnes's yard was unfenced, with nothing to decorate it this morning but a clothesline full of underwear.

He tied Sissy Belle to the Tolberts' picket fence and banged hard on the back door of the hardware store. When there was no answer, he banged harder.

"Stay," he said to Sissy Belle, and ran down the alley, around the block, and into the hardware store.

Mr. Tolbert was waiting on a roly-poly woman with three towheaded children who smelled like strawberry ice cream. Tres stood, first on one foot, then on another, and was getting ready to hand the money order to Mr.

Tolbert when he heard a commotion coming from behind the store.

"Whoo-ee! Whoo-ee!" a woman shouted over and over. Sissy Belle's unmistakable throaty hum interrupted her.

"Oh, no!" Tres said, hitting his forehead with the palm of his hand.

His mind slammed into gear as he ran through the store to the back door, Mr. Tolbert right behind him.

Sissy Belle had backed away from the fence as far as the reins allowed her. She stood trembling, bug-eyed with fear. A clump of Mrs. Tolbert's limp snapdragons hung from her pursed lips.

"That critter ate a whole row of my flowers. It's going to pull the fence down now," Mrs. Tolbert snapped. She flapped her arms like a bird trying to take off.

The roly-poly woman from the store, red-faced now, kept clicking her tongue and saying, "If this don't beat all!"

Tres wanted to brain her.

The fence leaned forward dangerously. Tres grabbed the reins off it and swung into the saddle. He thrust the money order at Mr. Tolbert, whose mouth was gaping open.

"I'm sorry, ma'am," Tres said to Mrs. Tolbert. "This mule is a pure pain. I'll get her out of your way."

Sissy Belle crab-stepped forward. Mrs. Tolbert, her face a furious red, waved her flowered apron in the mule's face and hollered "Whoo-ee!" again.

"Don't do that, ma'am," Tres pleaded.

Sissy Belle laid her ears back, clamped her tail down,

and bucked off into Sheriff Barnes's yard. Tres pulled on the reins and tried to turn her before she hit the clothesline, but he was in a sea of baby-blue slips, pink underwear, and plaid jockey shorts before he knew what hit him.

It occurred to him that they might have stayed there, turning in confused circles, forever, but a little rat terrier ran off the back porch, yipping at them.

Sissy Belle bucked through the laundry, a pair of enormous pink underpants caught on her ears, and took off down the alley, with the rat terrier chasing them. Tres held on tight, pulling hard on the reins as they went. She finally came to a screeching whoa just before they got to the street at the end of the alley.

Tres turned in the saddle and watched the rat terrier trot back down the alley, wagging its tail. He realized that his knees were shaking.

"Are you okay?" a familiar voice called from the street corner.

His heart was beating like a drum, and he felt his ears flush red. She could be anywhere in the great big world right now, and she's got to be twenty feet away, he thought.

"I'm still alive, ain't I?"

Robin Welch walked up the street toward him, grinning. "I like the hat. It's real cute."

Tres looked down and saw that the pink underpants were still on Sissy Belle's ears.

"Oh, great." His voice cracked. He jerked the pants off Sissy Belle's head and shoved them in his back pocket.

He got off the mule and stood in front of her, trying to look casual.

"What on earth is that?" Robin asked, pointing at Sissy Belle.

Think fast, Bomer, Tres told himself.

"Don't you know?" he asked at length.

"I'm the one asking," she said, and tossed her head proudly.

"It's a mean killer mule."

"It doesn't look mean."

"Well, that's just a case of looks deceiving. Heck, this mule kicked our rankest bull in the head. Killed him, too," Tres said.

"No."

"Oh, yes. We can't keep her around children, either. She tries to eat 'em." He narrowed his eyes.

"Tres Bomer! She's practically asleep." Robin started to giggle.

"That's when you've really got to watch her. Pretty soon she'll breathe fire out of both nostrils and metamorphose into Godzilla."

"Tell me the truth." She reached a hand slowly forward to touch Sissy Belle, but jerked it back when the mule snorted.

"Truth is, she ain't worth a box of rocks, and I'd rather herd goats than ride her," he said bitterly.

Sissy Belle shifted her weight to the other hip and wheezed.

"Aw, I think she's all right. Why are you riding her if you don't like her?" Robin asked.

"My granddaddy's trying to build my character, is all I can figure. If it was up to me, I'd have the sicko put away."

On impulse, Tres told Robin about Mariah and the heifer and the deal he'd struck with Senior. She was so easy to talk to that he told her about Mrs. Tolbert's flowers and Sheriff Barnes's clothesline.

She laughed out loud, her wonderful laugh. Watching her, Tres felt his heart turn over.

"This ain't the first time I've been feelin' bad and you come along and cheer me up," Tres said. "I think you like me," he teased.

"I'm always nice to little kids." She looked away for a moment and then gave him the full wide-eyed effect of her blue, blue eyes. "Give me those underpants, and I'll take them back to Mrs. Barnes," she offered, holding her hand out.

"Would you? It was a real stink back there. I couldn't face it right now." He handed her the pink pants.

She walked up the alley and smiled back at him.

"Thanks," he called. His heart felt like a melted candle.

He maneuvered Sissy Belle across the street to the railroad tracks. They went back up the lonely careening little road to the farm-to-market blacktop.

The wind changed direction, and suddenly the sky was flat as a cookie sheet. Clouds the color of charcoal pressed down close. A network of sheet lightning spread through the clouds, followed by a low rumbling in the west. Rain was close enough that Tres could smell it on the wind.

He didn't mind. He didn't have far to go, and besides, he was dizzy with happiness as he rode along the fence-line. Robin Welch liked him, he was working toward getting the prettiest mare in Wooster County, and he was a born roper. Everything seemed possible.

A red Buick convertible shot past him, going toward Summit. He heard the brakes screech and looked behind him to see the car back up. It came blazing around them, throwing up a choking cloud of dust. Tack was driving, and Coot turned around in his seat and stared at Tres, his face frozen in surprise.

five

*E*mbarrassment shot through Tres like lightning, followed by a rush of heat. He felt his face grow pink. Kicking Sissy Belle hard, he kept going.

"Ride 'em, cowboy!" Tack hollered, backing the car to keep pace with Tres as he went forward.

Tack waved his hat in the air. "You cut a dashing figure on that fine-looking animule. Get it? Ani*mule*?" He laughed so hard tears rolled down his cheeks.

"Shut up, Tack," Tres snapped.

"Say, you could hang your hat on that mule's hipbones; use her for a hatrack," Tack continued, and slapped his leg.

"Very funny. Is the quarter horse still for sale?"

"Not for long, Tres ol' buddy. I've had a lot of offers." Tack gunned the motor, and the red car took off like the wind, leaving twin patches of rubber.

Tres was unable to put into words to himself the mixture of shame and hurt he felt. Coot hadn't even told Tack to lay off. He'd just sat there with his mouth wide open.

"Best friends, huh, Coot? Some best friend you are," Tres muttered.

He rode along, wishing he'd told Coot to shut his mouth or the flies might get in.

Sissy Belle snorted and shied toward the fenceline, almost hanging Tres's jeans in barbed wire.

"Get over, you old fool," Tres growled, kicking her.

Panic surrounded him like the dark sky. The hoorawing was bad enough, but worse than that, his carefully laid plans suddenly seemed full of complications.

He had a bargain with Granddaddy, sure. But even if he kept to his end and delivered the heifer for sale, there was no guarantee Mariah would still be around. She could sell any day, and this was the fact he'd been refusing to face. A sandbag seemed to drop on his chest.

He was startled when Sissy Belle stopped abruptly and sat down in the road like a dog.

"Get up!" Tres ordered, and put his heel to her belly.

Sissy Belle wouldn't budge. He slid off the saddle, tried tugging her to her feet with the reins, but she sat placidly by the side of the road.

"Git!" Tres yelled. "I ain't gonna put up with anything weird."

He popped her rump with a chinaberry switch, but she just turned and looked at him with soulful eyes.

A gust of wind blew, shaking the brush. A zigzag of lightning danced across the sky, followed by cold raindrops as big as cherries. Next thing Tres knew, it was coming down in sheets, and there wasn't a place in sight to take cover. He made one last attempt to push Sissy Belle from behind.

Tears of frustration burned his eyes as he took off toward the ranch in a run, his hands curled into fists. A few yards down the road, he slipped in the wet mud and looked back. He could barely make her out through the rain, but he could have sworn the mule was asleep.

Tres took a hot shower when he got home. Senior and Junior were in the barn doing chores, and he was glad to have the house to himself.

Frustration made him so clumsy that he buttoned his shirt all wrong and had to start at the bottom and go up.

The rain stopped drumming on the roof, and he looked out the window, to see Sissy Belle joggling up the road as if nothing had ever happened.

Tres slammed the kitchen door so hard that it rattled on its hinges. He jerked the saddle off Sissy Belle's back and pulled her into a stall. Grabbing a towel, he roughly dried her off. He considered kicking one of her knobby knees.

"You look madder'n a rained-on rooster, Tres," Senior said, leaning on the stall door. Junior came out from the tack room with saddle soap on his hands.

"This ol' mule sulled up and left me stranded on the highway in the storm," Tres said crossly. He went on to tell about Mrs. Tolbert's flowers and Sheriff Barnes's clothesline.

"She's unpredictable. She's undependable, too, and she's so weird-lookin' most folks don't even know she's a dang mule, Granddaddy."

"She just had a fit of mischief is all," Senior said.

"She's ridiculous, Granddaddy. For God's sake."

"Don't blaspheme," Senior said. "May the whole town do the jitterbug in hell before I stand around and listen to you bellyache." And he walked out of the stable.

Unable to keep his doubts to himself any longer, Tres turned to Junior. "I tell you, I've got to wonder if this is worth it, Daddy. It's not just what she did today. She's afraid to cross even the narrowest part of Slaughter Creek. It took me three days last week to figure out that you have to turn her around in a circle before she'll splash on through."

"For a wonder," Junior said, as though he'd just heard an amazing piece of information.

"The most aggravatin' thing is this: We'll be goin' along just fine, and all of a sudden she just backs up, like your old pickup when you throw it in reverse. She never goes far, but there's no rhyme or reason for it.

"Meanwhile, Tack Taylor's over there trying to sell that mare every hour of every day, and Coot's goin' to give me a hard time all week at school because he got a look at Sissy Belle." Tres felt tired and ragged.

"You didn't tell Coot about Sissy Belle?"

"I was too embarrassed at first to tell anyone. I would have gotten around to it."

"At least the heifer's behaving herself," Junior offered.

"But for how long? It's so complicated, like a puzzle

51

almost. If all the pieces fit together just right, I'll get the mare. If even one little piece is missing, that's it."

They stood in an unhappy silence. For a terrible moment Tres was afraid Junior might say something fatherly, like "That's the way life is, son."

Instead, he announced, "Tres, I been aimin' to talk to you for a while now." He stopped and searched Tres's face. "Well, forget it for now," he said at length. "Oh, heck. You want a piece of peach pie with ice cream on top?"

TRES spent an uncomfortable week feeling confused and mad at the world. What had begun to occur to him was this: Maybe it was better not to ever want anything too much. Where did you put your wants if you didn't get the thing you wanted? Maybe wanting Mariah was just some grandiose pie-in-the-sky dream.

At night, when Tres lay down and shut his eyes, he followed Tack. In his mind, he went with him past the big sign with the horse on top, which said TAYLOR HORSE RANCH.

He followed him to the Taylors' big white house, where the windows were yellow with light. Inside, he saw the shadowy room where Mr. Taylor sat at night, reading the paper in front of a fireplace so big you could roast a steer in it.

Upstairs, the mother sat in her bedroom, warm and glowing, in front of a dressing table with rows of crystal jars. She called Tack "darling," she always had, hard as it was to understand why.

Tres followed Tack out to the horse barns, where Mariah waited, saddled and bridled. He watched Tack ride into the night, and it made his chest hurt.

After the rainstorm, the weather turned cold. There was a thin layer of snow on the ground every morning, and by late afternoon it had turned to ice. The sky was the same drab color of gray every day, and a sharp wind whistled around the corners of the house while Tres practiced his throws in the morning.

On Monday, there was a sign on the message board at school, where he couldn't miss it: *Mule crazy? Me, too. Call me and we'll talk about it. Tres.*

Tack had used red ink, and the loops and lassos of his longhand scrawled across the page.

Tres yanked it down and stuffed it in the trash can. He felt as if everyone stared at him when he walked down the hall, but no one said anything.

Robin was out of school four days in a row, and Tres was let down every single one of them. He hurried to his classes when he saw Coot's red head moving toward him in the hall. He felt wronged by Coot, and he didn't feel like being teased or even questioned about Sissy Belle.

He ate lunch in the science lab every day with Bubba Wayne, who was in a brood of his own. They stared at cows' eyes floating in jars, and Bubba told him about a different tropical disease every day.

On Friday, Tres slouched at the laboratory table, his cheek propped on his fist in a slipshod manner. His spirits were at zero. The air in the lab was thick with formaldehyde fumes. He stared at a pile of dissected frogs by the sink. They had been emptied out, squeezed of every drop of vitality. That's how I feel, he thought, munching on an apple.

"In the jungles of South America they have these green attack bugs," Bubba said. "They lie down on you when you least expect it, and gnaw on you for a while. Then they poop next to the sore. When you scratch, it goes right into your bloodstream. Pretty soon you come down with Mugre's disease."

All of Bubba's stories ended the same way.

Tres sighed. "And then you die."

"Yep. And then you die."

Tres glanced at the door. It must be time for the bell to ring, he thought. Kids were slamming their lockers and filing in and out of the bathrooms across the hall.

Robin walked past the door. She turned her head and caught his eye as she went. She backed up and came into the room.

"It stinks in here!" she said, waving a hand in front of her nose.

"Where have you been?" Tres asked, his heart leaping.

"I had some kind of bug," she said.

"Come here and let me see your eyes," Tres commanded.

Robin came forward and opened her blue eyes wide.

"Oh, Lord," he said, and looked at Bubba in mock horror. "Changosis."

"What are you talking about?" Robin put her hands

on her hips. She had on hot-pink socks that matched her sweater.

"That's no bug you had. It's worms. See, a fly must have bit you and laid its eggs in your bloodstream. When they hatch, they're these gross little white worms. They wiggle all the way up to your eyeballs. They're right on your eyeball there. I can see them wiggling around," Tres said, making a face.

"Is this a joke?" she asked. "What's the punch line?" She sat down in the chair across from him.

"No, listen. There's a lot of this around right now," Tres said seriously, warming to his subject. "These flies flew in from South America. Bubba's been telling me about it all week."

"What else?" she asked, her eyes as big as a rabbit's.

God, I like you, he thought. He smiled at her, trying to send a thought message, while Bubba chimed in.

"Well, there's several cases of bog fever. See . . ."

The bell rang, and they walked down the hall, listening to Bubba talk about the hallucinations that were part and parcel of bog fever. Tres couldn't believe he was walking right in front of everyone with Robin Welch. He was glad she was looking at Bubba, so that he could look at her. She had a little gold ring on her finger, with a heart dangling from it.

Oh, Lord, I am sick in love, he thought, and ran smack into Coot Taylor as they turned the corner.

"Bomer! I've been lookin' for you everywhere. Tack left town this morning for the weekend, and he ain't sold the mare yet. If you come over this afternoon you can ride her. We could do a little hunting, cook out, that kind of thing." Coot's eyebrows shot up while he waited for an answer.

"You bet!" Tres said. Every bit of the anger he'd felt toward Coot all week drained out of him as he thought about riding Mariah.

Robin smiled and waved at him as she walked off down the hall.

Tres wasn't good for anything until they got off the bus at Coot's ranch. He was twisting with impatience. It seemed to take Coot far too long to put his books up and get a couple of shotguns. Coot grabbed a Coke bottle and filled it with a package of peanuts, which seemed to fall through the glass in slow motion. Even the phone call Tres made to Junior was agonizingly long.

Coot saddled the mare and his black gelding, Johnny, while Tres watched.

"She's all yours," Coot said, standing back from Mariah.

Tres tightened the mare's girth and settled into the saddle. Mariah nickered at Johnny. Tres noticed that her ears were pricked up and her tail was held high. She feels as good as I do, he thought.

They turned up the collars of their jackets and walked the horses through the icy fields toward the trees on the western side of the property. Coot jogged slowly forward when they hit the woods, and Tres followed. Flakes of snow drifted down through the trees and settled on Coot's red hair, making it look as though it had been dusted with powdered sugar.

Everything's pretty, Tres thought. The whole world looks different on this horse. I have to see everything and smell everything and remember it all. It may have to last me a long time.

He'd been miserable all week, trying to prepare himself in case things didn't work out. But he'd given himself over the first time he'd seen Mariah, and he didn't know how to take himself back. I'll get her no matter what, he thought.

They rode through pockets of freezing air, the only sound the crunching of the horses' hooves on the crisp ice and the swish-swosh of the saddle. Tres saw a clearing of frozen mesquite grass up ahead and shifted his weight forward. Mariah moved into a smooth, slow gallop, keeping her head low. Tres touched her with his heels and moved her into an all-out run. She was stretched out low to the ground, her mane flying in the wind.

After riding Sissy Belle, Tres felt as if he were tearing around a racetrack. Mariah never broke step until they circled the field twice and he reined her in beside Coot.

"I think I'm in nirvana, or whatever it is they call it," Tres said. "She's smooth. Tack hasn't messed her up yet."

"That's because he's almost given up messin' with her at all. She dumps him every time he gets on her. Tack can outwit people, but he can't outwit livestock. Weird, isn't it?"

"How come she hasn't sold yet?" Tres asked.

"Don't know. But come spring and roundup time, people are goin' to be buying. You sure look good on that mare, Tres."

"Thanks, Coot," Tres said, but Coot's words were like a stitch in his side.

"Let's hunt before it gets too dark. I've got some matches and my buck knife. All we need is a couple of cotton-tails, and we'll have a feast," Coot said.

Tres agreed, although the only thing he really wanted to do was ride Mariah. They tied the horses in a stand of trees and walked for a quarter of a mile until they found some brown, pea-sized droppings and tracks leading to a brush pile.

Tres headed up the pile, while Coot stood a few yards off. Tres jumped up and down for a few seconds, until a gray cottontail bolted from a hole in the pile. Coot threw the shotgun to his shoulder, fired, and missed.

"Dang!" Coot said.

They walked along a frozen creekbed.

"There's a regular rabbit hotel here. The bunnies hide from the wind in the overhang," Coot said. "You do the shooting from now on. You're a better shot, any-way."

"Nah. You've just gotta aim ahead of him, Coot. That way he'll head into the shot."

Coot's voice droned on and on, and Tres tried to think about Mariah and all the things he'd do if she were his. He'd train her slow and easy, maybe use a snaffle bit and a tie-down. He'd save his money for a roping sad-dle, and start her out on slow calves.

He couldn't enjoy his thoughts. For all Coot's talking, Tres felt an unspoken question in the air.

"Look, about the mule . . . ," Tres began.

"Never mind. I'm sorry Tack carried on so," Coot said. "To be perfectly truthful, when I saw you on that animal, I'm like . . ." Coot looked bewildered.

"Well, she's a mule, and there ain't many around anymore."

"That ain't just a mule, Tres. That's a vision of hell," Coot said.

Tres felt the afternoon begin to sour. His granddaddy and Sissy Belle were hard facts of life he had to deal with, and he didn't know how to explain them to someone who had never had a hardship.

"Look, Coot, it ain't like it is with your parents. Senior won't give in without a fight, and the mule's the fight."

"Kind of like a trial by fire, huh?" Coot stopped on the icy creekbed, gun in hand, and looked at Tres.

"That's a pretty accurate description."

Tres looked down, trying to think of something more to say, and saw a crouched rabbit, three feet to the left of Coot's boot. Coot's eyes followed Tres's, and he pointed to it.

"Blast it," Tres said. He was busting to laugh, but he kept a straight face.

"I can't. It's too close to us," Coot whispered, his face flushed red as a Crayola.

"Okay, poke it with your gun, and shoot it when it jumps up," Tres whispered.

Coot prodded the cottontail with the barrel of the shotgun. It didn't move. He prodded it again, harder.

"It won't move," Coot whispered, lifting his free hand, as though at a loss for a solution. "It's terrified!"

"Reach down and grab it by the neck. Be careful it don't bite you, Coot. You could get rabies, you know."

Slowly, Coot bent over. He reached carefully forward until his hand gripped the rabbit's neck. It still didn't move when Coot held it up, a bewildered look on his face. It was frozen stiff.

Tres fell on the ground, laughing, waving his feet in the air. "Stiff as a poker, dead as a doornail," he sputtered.

Coot dropped the dead rabbit, and it thumped down the frozen creekbed.

"You ain't aiming to tell anybody about this, are you?" Coot asked. His face was red clear to his ears.

"Who, me?" Tres grinned at the thought and threw his free arm over Coot's shoulder. He turned in the direction of the horses. "You know, Coot, being your best friend don't mean I have to volunteer for target practice. You and your brother get off my back about my ugly mule."

six

*B*y the middle of February, the sun was climbing high and hot in the sky every day, and the RC Cola thermometer on the porch showed that the temperature had reached seventy-five all week and even eighty one day. Tres couldn't remember when they'd ever had such a warm spell in the winter. That's Texas, he thought. If you don't like the weather one day, just stick around and watch it change the next.

One evening after dinner, Tres passed his granddaddy's room. Senior sat in a chair, carefully unfolding his newspaper in the little pool of light cast by his reading lamp. He seemed to fill the room.

"Tres," he said. "I'm goin' to a ranch outside of Presidio to look at a bull on Saturday. I need your daddy to drive me."

"Yes, sir," Tres said.

"Well, you know what that means, don't you? You'll

have to be in charge here from early morning to close to midnight. Is that a problem for you?" Senior asked.

"No problem at all, Granddaddy." Actually, it could be a problem, and Tres knew it. The list of things that could go wrong in one day on a ranch were endless. Yet he couldn't help the deep feeling of pride that washed over him when he realized that his granddaddy trusted him that much.

"Now, look-a-here. That means no lollygagging around. There'll be lots of chores to get done. No yammering on the phone." Senior began to check his instructions off with his right finger on his left thumb.

He stood up in the half dark, still going through his list of don'ts. He smelled of soap and tobacco. Suddenly, he reached a big hand toward Tres, who ducked back on impulse. Tres thought he was going to take a fistful of his shirt at the throat and threaten him with a beating if he messed up.

Senior's old face fell. "Just wanted to ruffle your hair, son." The effect on Senior was embarrassing. His face flushed, and he looked stung.

Tres walked out, biting his lip so hard it almost brought tears to his eyes. He wished he could do worse. Bang his head against the wall, bite a chunk out of his leg.

ANOTHER bright, hot sun came up on Saturday morning. Tres expected another long list of instructions, but Senior just frowned at him from the pickup.

"You're in charge, son. Don't idle."

Tres spent a busy Saturday mucking out stalls in the

barn and stacking new bales of hay until his shoulders hurt. He loaded the old pickup with hay to scatter for the cattle in the morning. He knew that his granddaddy wouldn't comment on all the work he'd done, but he'd notice it for sure. He'd also notice if something went wrong.

Tres wanted to please Senior, and he worked clear through lunch. By midafternoon his stomach felt empty and sick. He went to the kitchen, opened the refrigerator, and let the cold air pour over him while he drank a quart of milk straight out of the carton.

He grabbed a lunch bag Junior had left him and saddled Sissy Belle. When they got to the edge of Slaughter Creek, she stopped abruptly. Tres kicked her twice before he turned her in a circle. She still wouldn't splash through.

He didn't kick her anymore or yell at her, for fear she'd sull up and refuse to go at all. At least he had her on her feet, and that was where he wanted to keep her.

"Go on. Be as muleheaded as you please. We've got plenty of time to check the herd, and I'm going to eat and take a nap. Just watch me." Tres climbed out of the saddle and pulled his lunch bag off the saddle horn.

He sat down by the side of the creek where strong new grass poked up in spots, and a couple of brown lizards scattered. The milky green water in the creek ran over the rocks, cold and fast.

He pulled a steak sandwich wrapped in waxed paper from the bag and stuck a can of Coke in the creek to chill. While Sissy Belle cropped grass under a tree, he wolfed his sandwich down and ate some of Junior's famous lemon snaps. He drank the Coke, put his hat over his eyes, and was asleep in two winks.

Tres heard the first distant bawl in his sleep. He jerked quickly awake, aware that something was wrong. He sat up and listened. The sun was getting low, and it was the quiet hour of the day, before deer time. Even so, it seemed too quiet, and it scared him some. It reminded him of all the old cowboy movies he'd ever seen on television. There was always a dead still spell before the Indians swooped down from the hills and scalped everybody.

Sissy Belle jingled her bridle bit, making him jump; and then he heard the bellow again. He'd been around cattle long enough to be able to tell by the tone whether the bawling was coming from a cow, a steer, or a bull. This was a cow, and the bawl was long and low and deep. It was a peculiar sound, not at all like a mother bawling for her calf to answer, or a stray lost from the herd.

Tres jerked Sissy Belle's reins up. He pulled her through the icy stream without giving her time to think, and mounted her. He got her into a slow trot and headed downstream in the direction of the sound. He rode a mile or so, the sun directly in front of him, going slowly down, before he located the herd, milling around a salt lick.

The bawling was a deep-gutted, wretched cry now, and he followed it to a brushy draw. Tres lit down and tied Sissy Belle to a mesquite tree. He hadn't realized until now that he was breathing hard, and his heartbeats felt like club blows in his chest.

He walked up the draw a ways until he found his heifer. He'd been hoping it was one of the others, but he told himself he should have known, he should have known. She lowered her head and swung it from side to side. She was white-eyed, and strings of foamy slobber flew from her mouth.

Tres stood stock-still, a knot of terror growing in his chest. He felt that he could smell the danger, stirring on the wind.

"What's wrong, girl?" His voice broke and sounded hoarse to his own ears.

At first, he thought she must have been bit by a hydrophobic dog, though it didn't make sense to him. Her upturned horns looked so threatening that he was afraid to move. He felt his legs begin to shake. She staggered into the brush, panting hard now, still bawling.

What's wrong? he wanted to scream. Mugre's disease? Bog fever? He heard himself laugh out loud, but it seemed to come from someone else. Oh, Lord, pull yourself together, Bomer. Don't freak now, he begged himself.

He took a few steps toward her. She swung her head but didn't seem to see him. He inched forward until he was directly in front of her. She didn't shy when he reached forward to touch her. Her neck was darkened with sweat, and she felt hot to his touch. Even her nose was dry and hot.

Closer now, he could see that she was standing on

three feet. Her lower right front leg was swollen more than twice its normal size.

Nothing was broken; Tres could see that clearly. He dropped to his knees to get a better look. Her leg muscles were quivering when he carefully took her foot in his hand.

A watery fluid tinged with blood seeped from a place on the heifer's foot, pasting down the hairs there. Tres was no longer afraid she'd use her horns on him, but a whole new fear made the hair lift on his neck. He was looking at puncture wounds, about a half inch apart. He'd seen them a couple of times before, when the ranch dogs had gotten rattlesnake bit in spring or summer.

"I'm goin' for Junior, girl. He'll know what to do," Tres said, looking into her face so close he could feel her hot breath.

He ran down the draw toward Sissy Belle, the rocks skittering beneath his boots. His shirt was soaked through with sweat, and his hat felt heavy on his head.

He was reaching for Sissy Belle's reins when he remembered that Junior would be in Presidio by now. The realization hit him like a blow to the chest, and he almost groaned at his stupidity.

I'll go to the house, call Dr. Sanders in town, he thought, his spirits lifting. He grabbed hold of the saddle horn and put a foot in the stirrup.

Stupid, stupid, stupid, he told himself again bitterly, as he stood with one foot in the stirrup and one foot on the ground. By the time the vet got to the house and we rode back out here, he thought, it would be pitch black. The heifer could wander off anywhere, be dead, even.

He buried his head in Sissy Belle's neck. The back of his shirt was drenched. He could feel sweat trickling down his sides.

"I'm goin' to wake up any minute now. It's just a bad dream, anyways," he murmured to Sissy Belle.

He felt desolate, blocked in every direction. He was finished. Done. It was all beyond him.

The heifer bellowed and left the brush in an awkward, heavy limp, her udders swinging.

If ever a creature needed help, she does, and you're a durned nitwit, Tres said to himself harshly. It was the sort of thing Senior would say. He thought it was funny— not funny ha-ha but peculiar—that he would think of Senior now. It occurred to him that maybe it was because Senior would do something, even the wrong thing, before he'd be hopeless and behave like a sissy.

He sat down under Sissy Belle to think, casting back in his memory for all he knew about snakebite. It was a rattlesnake bite, he was certain it was because she had that same musky odor he remembered on the dogs, and her pain and swelling were so bad. The quicker he acted, the better chance she'd have.

Years back, he'd watched Junior use a tourniquet and make a couple of cuts on a dog's leg that had been bitten. He'd sent Tres to the refrigerator for ice cubes, and they'd packed them around the swelling to keep the poison from spreading. Tres felt downcast for a moment, remembering that the dog had died anyway. Still, a cow was bigger than a dog and stood a better chance.

He took a rope from his saddle. The sun was almost down, but the sky still held its light. He'd build a big fire by the stream in case the moon didn't cast enough light.

The heifer had quit bellowing for the time being, but she still swung her head from side to side, making it hard for Tres to fasten the loop around her neck. He finally tugged her down to the edge of the water, where he tied her to a chinaberry tree. He built a fire with dry leaves and dead branches from a mesquite tree.

He pulled his shirt off and ripped one of the sleeves away at the shoulder seam to make a tourniquet. He tied it a few inches above the bite, to limit the spread of the venom.

"Fifteen minutes on, two minutes off," he muttered. "Or is it the other way around?" Panic seized him, but he decided the first made more sense.

He took his pocket knife out and opened the blade. He held it over the flames of the fire to sterilize it.

Tres took the heifer's foot in his left hand and held his breath. His hand shook, while her foot quivered. There was a metallic taste in his mouth.

"Oh, Lord, I hope I know what I'm doing," he said, not at all sure that he did.

He made a short cut over each fang mark to relieve the pressure and let the poison drain out. Dark blood seeped from the wound.

He quickly pulled off his boots and socks. The heifer panted heavily as he led her into the water, hock deep.

Melt-off from the snow and ice a couple of weeks back had left the creek freezing cold and bank full. The shock of the cold water knocked his breath out. The cow didn't want to stay, and reared back toward the creekbank, knocking Tres backward into the icy water. He grabbed the rope and managed to pull her back in.

Tres was afraid her temperature had spiked in the last few minutes. He splashed water over her shoulders and neck until it was time to take off the tourniquet. His arms and legs felt numb and shaky.

Tres glanced up, to see that the light was gone from the sky and a lemon-yellow moon was perched just above the ridge. The heat from the sun was gone, and the night air was cold. He shivered and looked longingly at the fire.

Tres turned back toward the heifer, his teeth chattering. Again he tied the tourniquet on and washed her down with cold water, trying to lower her temperature.

The night wore on and on, a solid round of cold water and remembering to tie and untie the tourniquet. He left the water from time to time to put more wood on the fire and warm himself up, but the heifer followed him out each time. It got harder and harder to go back in the water, but Tres knew that he had to keep her foot cold and her temperature down.

seven

 *T*res didn't know how many hours had passed, but the moon was high in the sky. The heifer was calm now, though she was still panting, and the swelling looked about the same.

He sat on the squishy mud by the edge of the creek-bank, his back to the fire, and stripped his wet jeans off. He draped them by the fire to dry, and put the torn shirt back on. He pulled his knees up to his chest and rubbed a shaking hand across his mouth. The heifer was in shallow water, but her foot was still under. Air colder than a well-digger's elbow came off the water, but Tres was reluctant to move for fear the heifer would leave the creek.

He watched in anxious silence. She'll probably make it, but what if she loses the calf? he asked himself. Oh, Lord, don't think about it now. He studied the moon: anything to keep from thinking. The moon looked so close that he thought he could see the oceans and craters on it. The mesquite fire popped, and somewhere coyotes howled. They sounded as hungry and lonesome as Tres felt.

What if I've done the wrong things? What if she gets an infection in those cuts I made? he wondered. He counted backward from one hundred to one, a game he used to play when he wanted the time to pass.

Tres felt tired and bone cold. He had no idea how much time had passed or how long he'd sat there, when he heard a horse nicker. Sissy Belle snorted and stamped her foot.

Junior called him from downstream, a frantic note in his voice. Relief flooded through Tres, and tears stung his eyes.

"Down here, Daddy, I'm down here," he yelled. His teeth chattered so hard the words came out peculiar.

Tres heard Bess cross the creek and break into a gallop. Junior lit down when he got to the draw, and ran to Tres. He pulled off his down jacket and put it around Tres's shoulders. Tres had never seen his daddy move so fast.

"Thank God, Tres. I thought you were dead in a ravine somewheres."

"Check the heifer, Daddy. She's been rattlesnake bit, and I don't know if I done the right things, 'cept she seems better." Tres's words came out in a tumble as he told Junior about the past few hours. Junior pulled the heifer out of the water and examined her leg in the firelight.

"Sounds like a pretty close shave, but you did a good

job. We can move her up to the house at daylight. If we can get her to eat, she'll be all right. I'm more worried about you right now."

Junior put more mesquite branches on the fire. Sparks flew up. Tres moved in close to the fire, glad that Junior would take over for a while. He felt Junior's arm around him, tight and secure. He leaned into his daddy's shoulder, feeling it was the best place to be. The adrenaline that had kept him going all night seeped away, and he felt warm and drowsy. His feelings nagged him, though.

"Daddy, the whole time I've been out here with the heifer, I wasn't thinkin' of savin' her so that she could live. I was thinkin' that if I lost her, I'd lose the horse," Tres said.

"Yeah?"

"I kept thinkin' over and over that even if I pulled her through, she could lose the calf, and I might not make enough money without the both of them."

"Well, we ain't none of us sproutin' wings on this earth, honey," Junior said.

"It ain't no credit to me, because she's been like a pet to me," Tres said.

"Oh, don't look so blue. Mebbe it ain't no credit, but leastways it's human. Besides, you got her out of many a scrape before this, when there wasn't anything in it for you."

Tres felt better. It was true, but something else tugged at the corners of his mind.

"Daddy, maybe somebody's trying to tell me something. Not one thing havin' to do with gettin' this horse

72

has been easy. If every month is as long as the last one's been, I'll never get my whole life lived."

"Well, if there was anything easy in this life, you and me both know I'd of found it by now." A sheepish grin spread across Junior's face.

"Things are easy for Coot," Tres blurted.

"Aw, I wouldn't be so sure. Things are tough for you right now, and it hurts me that it's so. But Coot has Tack for a brother. That poor son of a buck leans toward a self-destructive style of life. He can't be easy to contend with."

"That's true."

"Anyway, he can't do what you can do neither."

"What's that?" Tres asked.

"Throw them hungry loops. Every one of your throws looks like the only one you'll ever get to make. Someday everybody's goin' to know your name," Junior said with pride.

"How come you never said nothin' before?"

"It scared me. I've been hearin' your granddaddy bad mouth the rodeo circuit all my life, but that's where you're headed someday," Junior said. "I've got used to the idea."

"Why does Granddaddy hate it so? He was good in his day."

"Fear. He just lost his nerve. It happens. You ride one too many boogery bulls and one day you wake up and can't do it no more. But he gave up on his dream, and it's made him hard and mean." Junior stood up and looked at the cow's foot again.

"You ever had a dream, Daddy?"

Junior was quiet so long that, at first, Tres thought he hadn't heard him.

"Shoot, I've had a lot of dreams. You were the only one that really worked out."

Junior hugged Tres to him and patted his arm. "I got one now, and I been tryin' to find a way to talk to you about it. Pop's Café in town is for sale, and I've worked out a way with the bank to buy it from him."

"You have?" Tres was amazed. He tried to imagine his daddy talking to the men at the bank, a suit on and his hair plastered down. Somehow he'd done it, but Tres couldn't get a clear picture of it.

He could see Pop's Café, though, with its neon sign blinking and flashing from the road. A tough old bald-headed geezer called not Pop but Webb owned it. The food wasn't very good, but with Junior there, it would be great.

"Well, that's good. It's so close you can practically walk home when you close at night," Tres said.

"That's just the thing," Junior said. An uncomfortable feeling came over Tres. Junior cracked his knuckles one by one and searched his son's face.

Tres felt a rush of confusion. "What do you mean? You ain't leavin' me alone out here with Granddaddy, are you?"

"He wouldn't let me take you, nohow, Tres. Besides, you can come to the café every day after school and eat a piece of pie. I plan to have six different kinds every day. I'll take you home after. That'll be my slow time of day, anyways."

"Ain't you goin' to ask me to live with you there?" Tres asked.

"I just told you he wouldn't let you go. I haven't even told him *I'm* going yet. I tried all the way to Presidio and back, but it was like my lips was stuck together. He kept sayin', 'What's wrong? Cat got your tongue?' Let's face facts. It just wouldn't work." Junior looked miserable.

"You're just scared of him, that's all," Tres hollered.

"You're not kidding."

"If I can't go, you can't leave, either, then," Tres said stubbornly. He felt four years old again and on the verge of having a fit.

"I ain't going to Dallas, Tres. I'm just goin' a few miles down the road. It's different with you, son. He respects you. If I stay here, I'll spin out the rest of my days bein' a no-'count and a go-fetch boy for your granddaddy."

Tres didn't want to admit it, but what Junior said made an awful kind of sense.

"Ain't much, Tres. But it's the only hope I got."

Silence grew between them and spread like a dark cloud. Tres felt too tired and sulky to talk it out. He wasn't used to Junior being certain about anything, but Tres sensed he wouldn't change his mind, and it scared him.

With the first light of dawn, Junior rode back to the ranch for the pickup and a trailer for the heifer. Tres rode Sissy Belle and pulled the heifer behind him to the road.

He felt a flickering of satisfaction with himself as he

saw Senior in the truck with Junior. It was comforting to see the anxious look on Senior's face turn to one of relief and pride.

Senior rubbed the silver stubble on his cheek with a big hand. "Well, what kind of nonstop nonsense has this heifer been into now?"

Tres told him about the night, while Senior examined the wound.

"You did a good job, boy. Now we need to keep down infection. Let's load her up."

They put her into a stall in the barn. Her swelling had gone down, and she lay on the clean hay and slept. Senior gave Tres a liniment to rub into the wound so that she wouldn't lose the flesh around it.

"Go on up to the house," Senior finally ordered. "I'll keep an eye on her while you get some rest."

Tres was grateful. He'd only been gone a few hours, but it felt like years. When he got to the house, he looked around his room. His heifer had almost died, his daddy was leaving, but his room was just as he'd left it. His four-poster bed was made, his fishing poles leaned against the wall, and his autographed picture of Roy Cooper hung on the closet door. He touched a book on his desk. *Webster's Collegiate Dictionary*, it said on the dust jacket. Inside was a copy of *Cowgirls Looking for Love*. He let the pages flip through his fingers. Coot had underlined the good parts in red. Tres felt his face flush.

He closed the book and went into the bathroom. After a shower, he pulled on a clean pair of jeans and a T-shirt. When he came out, the house smelled of home-made bread baking.

Tres was too keyed up to sleep. Too many things had happened, too many things were changing. Mostly, he didn't want to think about Junior leaving.

He set a saddle on his desk chair and sat on the bed with his legs crossed, roping the saddle horn. He threw the loop over and over, never missing the horn once. He felt hypnotized, throwing the rope, flipping it off the horn before the loop closed.

Junior came to his door several times during the day, but Tres pretended not to see him.

There was roast beef for dinner and mashed potatoes and green beans and homemade bread with butter and strawberry jam—all his favorite foods. Tres picked through his pile of mashed potatoes.

"What's the matter, boy? What call have you got to slump around the table this way? Your heifer's going to be fine in a few days." Senior's eyebrows puckered.

Tres looked at Junior, who stood up abruptly and started clearing the table.

"Hellation!" Senior continued. "The two of you is act-ing right peculiar. Did you fall on your heads last night?"

"I'm goin' out to the barn and sit with the heifer a spell, Granddaddy," Tres said, and slammed out the back door. He crossed the flagstone porch, his hands jammed into the back pockets of his jeans.

Outside, the air was soft and the evening sky was pink in the west. The barn was dark and quiet, and it smelled of horse manure and hay. Tres sat down by the heifer in her stall and stroked her nose. Her leg looked better than it had in the morning.

Sissy Belle poked her nose over the next stall and peered at him through the gloom.

"Bet that snake had nine, ten rattles at least," Tres said to her.

His spirits rose a little when he thought of last night's ordeal. He'd done everything that could be done, and he'd saved her. She'd be ready to calve in a couple of weeks, and with any luck, Mariah would still be waiting for him.

He returned to the house and sat on the back porch. Stars glittered in the sky. To Tres the night sky was a comfort. The stars hold true to their course, he thought. *They* don't change. If he watched the night sky long enough, he could see the heavens turn. Cassiopeia's throne would turn over, and Orion would walk from one horizon to the other.

And then a cloud skated across the moon, making it look like a bad-luck moon to Tres. You get up in the morning, and you never know what's going to happen, Tres thought.

He heard Junior's voice, low and patient, but he couldn't hear what Junior was saying. Suddenly, Granddaddy's angry voice boomed through the open kitchen window.

"You go and make these plans without sayin' Peat Turkey to no one. Since your mind's set and you're going, then go on," Senior said.

"Tonight?" Junior asked.

"No sense shilly-shallying."

"I was goin' to stay until you hired someone to take my place. At least until Tres is easy in his mind about it," Junior said. His voice sounded raw.

"I'll have Juarez over here in the morning. As for Tres, he'll be fine. Now git," Senior said, with a tone of finality.

This is really happening, Tres said to himself. He's not leaving next week or next month, but right now.

Even if Junior could take him, Tres had no wish to live in town. He just didn't want Junior to leave him, alone as a shooting star, and unprotected. His feelings ached in his throat, but he didn't want to cry. What would Junior do if I grabbed his hands and begged him not to go? he wondered.

"You *get* yourself in hand, and I mean you do it *on the double,*" he whispered harshly to himself.

On impulse, he went straight to the kitchen, relieved that no one was there. He got his school directory from a drawer, looked up the number, and called Robin Welch. His heart accelerated when she answered the phone.

"This is Tres. Tres Bomer," he said.

"Hi, Tres."

"There's a dance on the square Friday night. Well, they have it every year to raise money for the fire department. The whole town practically goes." His voice wasn't behaving right, and he wished he could start over.

"Are you all right?" she asked.

"No, as a matter of fact I ain't, but I'd be better if you

said you'd meet me at the square." There, he thought, and took a deep breath.

"Well, I don't know."

Tres thought he could hear the smile in her voice. Okay, I ain't in the mood to play around, but it works, so here goes, he decided.

"If you don't say yes, I'm goin' to tie a dead cat on the end of a string outside your bedroom window. Now and again it will hit the pane when the wind blows at night and scare you half to death."

"That . . . is . . . the . . . worst . . . thing . . . I . . . have . . . ever . . . heard." She spaced her words out slowly.

"Will you go?" he asked.

"Sure. I'll meet you there at seven. By the way, I was going anyway. See, you could have played it cool," she teased.

"Takes too much time, and it ain't what it's cracked up to be," Tres lied. The fact was, he had always wanted to be cool. He had even practiced a few times. But nothing ever came of it.

Tres went to his room and lay on top of the covers. He could hear Junior packing across the hall. He fell asleep quickly but awoke later when he heard Junior load Bess into the trailer. The moon was bright, and Tres watched through the window as Junior stuck a stick in his gas tank to see how much was there. The gauge had broken long ago. He pulled the hood up and fiddled with something for a long while. Tres knew that he was stalling, hoping they would come out and wish him well, say goodbye at least. The dogs emerged from under the porch steps and sniffed his pants legs and wagged their tails.

Junior finally walked over to the window. "Tres, try to understand. When you ain't so mad at me, please come to the café. Your granddaddy won't be wanting to see me out here for a spell."

Tres didn't answer. He realized that for once he and Senior were on the same side about something.

Junior drove off, his shirt sleeves flapping in the breeze. Tres watched until the greasy little pickup bounced over the pipes of the cattle guard. He lay in bed counting the few things Junior actually owned—a dilapidated pickup, a few clothes, and Bess.

eight

At first, he and Senior skated constantly on thin ice. Junior's name never came up, and Tres wasn't about to introduce the subject, for fear his grand-daddy's temper would snap like an old rattrap.

The house had never been spick-and-span, but Junior had always kept the beds made, the clothes picked up, and the dishes washed.

Everything was a mess now, and Tres had a hard time finding clean clothes after a few days. The beds looked as if a war had been fought in them, and the porch was strewn with the Summit *Bugle*.

Tres felt Junior's absence most in the kitchen, though. At any time of the day, Tres used to come in and find a skillet of smothered steak slowly cooking or a pot of Junior's spicy pinto beans bubbling on the stove. There was always a lemon meringue pie or a devil's food cake with thick icing on the counter.

Now the counter was littered with coffee grounds and burned toast, and there were no good smells in the house. Whenever Senior opened a can of beans, he'd take the empty to the back door, throw it in the air, and shoot it with his .45 pistol, putting a hole in it before it hit the ground. Once, Tres found him stooped over the sink, gloomily washing dishes, and he looked old and tired. Tres knew that he missed Junior, too, but he was too proud to do anything about it.

The only subject they felt comfortable with was the heifer. She was in a pen now, and Senior thought that Tres should be thinking of putting her out to pasture again. It had always been his granddaddy's theory that cows calved better when they weren't watched. Tres wasn't sure, and it gave them something safe to argue about.

Senior hired a skinny Indian man named Juarez. He was the color of a coffee bean, and he had long, sinewy muscles, a high-cheeked face with a sharp nose, and thick long black hair.

Tres tried to be friendly. When attempts at ordinary conversation didn't work, he'd ask questions.

"Where's the new rope, Juarez?"

"Troca," he grunted.

"How's my heifer, Juarez?"

"Quién sabe?" Juarez spat.

"Had a nice day, Juarez?"

Juarez wiped his nose with the back of his hand and curled his lip.

Tres suspected that he had the temper of a hot tamale, but what Juarez lacked in personality he made up for in ability. He rode a gray Appaloosa light and easy as the wind. He knew immediately which cattle had strayed where and what to do about it. He mended fences without gloves, mucked stalls without a break, and fixed the windmill without new parts. For no good reason Tres could figure, he liked Juarez, but the man was no companion.

The school bus passed Pop's Café every morning on the way into town and again on the way out. Junior's pickup was always parked in front, and there was a sign in the window that read CLOSED FOR REPAIRS.

There were stacks of lumber and big silver paint cans littering the parking lot in front all week. By Friday, a brand-new blue-and-green neon sign was flashing JUNIOR'S TIP TOP CAFÉ.

The sign shocked Tres like a blow to the face. Junior had changed the name, added his own. For the first time, he realized that Junior wasn't coming back. Part of him wanted to see Junior, but the other part wanted to keep his back turned. That was the part that won out.

After school, Tres put on his new pearl-buttoned shirt and walked over to the town square with Coot.

"I bet you're goin' to spend the whole night dancin' with Robin Welch, or tryin' to, anyway," Coot said when they'd found a spot on the grass to sit.

"Course I am," Tres said.

"Shoot, you're hopeless." Coot looked disgusted and rolled his eyes heavenward.

Tres knew Coot had had a miserable time with girls.

They'd been teasing him about his red hair and freckles since he was a little biddy, and he'd never even found a girl he could be friends with.

At the school Christmas dance, Coot had finally gotten up his nerve to ask Debbie Barnes to dance. After it was over, she told all the other girls that Coot had sweaty palms.

"Debbie Barnes is a snot, Coot," Tres offered. "Ask one of the other girls to dance tonight."

"I wouldn't ask one of 'em for a ride if I was stranded in the middle of the Mojave Desert. I wouldn't ask them to save me if I was drownin' in the Dead Sea. If I was stuck on top of the Himalaya Mountains and one flew over in a helicopter, I swear I'd rather crawl down with two broken legs than ask one for a ride," Coot said. His face was as red as if he'd been swimming in the creek all day.

"Well, at least you know your geography," Tres pointed out.

They spent the rest of the afternoon flipping their pocket knives into the dirt of the flower beds and watching the firemen put up the food stands. There was a stand for hot dogs and hamburgers, another for flour tortillas with chicken and beef fajitas. There were beer and wine and soft-drink stands, and later the concession people came in with snow cone machines and popcorn.

The Summit Garden Club hung pink and green crepe-paper streamers across the gazebo in the center of the square. At dusk, Johnny Barr and the Two-Steps positioned themselves in the gazebo and tuned their guitars in the glow from the lights strung around the dance floor. Tres felt his spirits lift.

He ate a corn dog, careful not to get mustard on his shirt. By full dark, the square was alive with people laughing and calling to each other. Johnny Barr sang in a heavily accented two-beat:

> *Darlin', you killed my only thrill,*
> *Since you don't love me anymore.*

Couples pressed close on the dance floor. They glided bent-kneed, stepping together ahead of the beat. They hesitated as the beat caught up, rocked back on their heels, and turned and turned and turned.

Tres loved the tricky Texas country dancing. He tried to look casual as he searched for Robin in the crowd, but he felt nervous and jittery. He lost Coot and was about to look on the other side of the square, when he saw Tack on the edge of the dance floor with Robin.

He stood back in the shadows, out of sight. Tack was trying to teach her the two-step. Her face flushed as she watched her feet, and she looked up from time to time at Tack and laughed nervously.

Tres moved back farther. For a time, he'd thought that Robin really liked him. Now, seeing her with Tack, it seemed a fantasy he'd made up to entertain himself.

He considered cutting in, but he knew that if Tack

was in the wrong mood, Tres would end up on the ground, looking at the Big Dipper.

When the dance was over, Robin smiled and started to merge with the crowd. Tack pulled her back and moved her awkwardly into another dance before the music started again. She looked flustered.

Tres went to the hamburger booth and borrowed a pencil and paper and wrote down some words. He moved through the crowd and handed the paper up to the fiddle player on the gazebo.

At the end of the song, Johnny Barr took the note.

"First, I've got a lost child up here, name of Wally Perk, who wants his mama," Johnny said into the microphone. He lifted a snuffling little boy down to a couple on the dance floor.

"And let's see, here," Johnny continued. "I got a note here says, 'Robin Welch, your daddy and five brothers are hoppin' mad. Meet them at the first-aid station, where that ol' boy you're dancin' with is going to end up when they get through with him.' "

The crowd roared, and Johnny moved right into the strains of "Your Cheating Heart."

The first-aid station was a card table under a tree at the edge of the square. It was outside the glow of light, and there was no one in charge of it. A box of Band-Aids lay on the table.

Tres sat down in the chair behind the table and waited. He tried to be calm, to just sit there at the first-aid station as if that were his volunteer job for the night. But in fact he was a nervous wreck, and he flipped Band-Aids back and forth across the table. Someone finally came up behind him and laid cool hands over his eyes, knocking his hat off.

"Guess who?" she asked.

"The bad girl with five brothers?" he asked back. His heart banged in his chest, and he had a hard time swallowing.

Robin sat down on the grass and wound her arms around her knees. She had on a red sweater and a blue-jeans jacket. Her eyes were shining, and her cheeks were pink. Tres couldn't imagine anyone looking prettier.

"Tres Bomer, I don't know whether to hit you or kiss you."

"Tack Taylor's a good seven years older than you, and meaner'n a scorpion. I think you should kiss me."

"On the other hand, everyone's going to be afraid of me now," she said, and gave him a sidewise look.

"Good," Tres said.

"Can you teach me how to dance like that? I mean, over here where no one can see?" she asked.

"Sure, but you have to loosen up. You can't be so stiff, like you were with Tack," he instructed.

He took her hand and pulled her to him. She looked embarrassed and stared at his shirt. His heart was beating hard. Thump, thump, thump. He fully expected her to see the pocket of his shirt jumping.

"Okay, just follow me. Take two long steps like this here, and then a half step, which is really just a step-close-step," he said.

She fumbled on the half step and got flustered and stamped her foot.

"I've been making that same mistake all night," she said, and frowned.

"Relax. There ain't no hurry. Besides, I probably couldn't do those dances you all did in Austin."

"You're nice," she mumbled.

"I've been trying to tell you." He brushed some hair out of her eyes and took her hand again. "Now take a deep breath. That's what I do before I rope."

She wanted to move to the beat, and Tres showed her how to step ahead of it with him and wait. By the second song she was following him most of the time, and by the third, she was smiling again.

He didn't let her hand go after the song was over. They sat down under the tree and watched the other dancers, who seemed a million miles away to Tres.

Robin looked right at Tres and grinned. "You know," she said, "you're a very good dancer for a little kid."

"I ain't no little kid. Besides, you like me," Tres said. He felt an unstoppable impulse and put his hand on the side of her face and kissed her softly.

She didn't seem to mind, and he kissed her again.

"Hey, Bomer!" Coot stood by the first-aid table. "Sorry to bother you, but Junior's over to the beer booth, drunk as a hoot owl."

nine

"ho's Junior?" Robin asked.

Tres considered lying, but Coot stared him down.

"My father," Tres muttered. He stood, wishing the earth would open and gobble him up.

Robin opened her mouth in surprise.

"I better get him back to the café." He wanted to laugh it off, act as if it didn't matter, but he felt shamed in front of Robin. For a terrible moment he just stood there, exposed, aware that they were watching him.

"Tack and I'll pick you up at the café on the way home," Coot offered.

"Fine," Tres said. Though reluctant to leave, he walked into the glare of lights on the dance floor without looking back.

The puzzling thing to Tres was this: It wasn't like Junior

to get drunk in public. He'd always confined his drinking to bars, places where Tres wouldn't see him.

There were three beer stands. The crowd was so thick it was hard to get from one stand to the other. He passed Tack Taylor, standing in the shadows at the second one. Tack lit a cigarette off the one he'd just finished.

"There's some people in this crowd wound tight as a spring, just lookin' for a fight. Hell, five of 'em are lookin' fer me right now. It ain't turnin' out to be a good night. You know what I mean?" Tack asked.

"Yep, I sure do," Tres said, scanning the crowd for Junior.

What he saw next made his jaw clench. Junior was weaving his way up the gazebo steps, his stomach marching ahead of him.

He's going to sing, Tres thought. Right here in front of the whole town he's going to make a fool of all the Bomers, especially me.

Junior loved to sing sad love songs. He'd sung Tres to sleep with "Lying Eyes" when he was little, and he sang snatches of "Whiskey River" when he cooked dinner or doctored the animals. Thing was, Tres thought he had a pretty good voice, but to sing in front of all these people . . . ?

Junior crossed the gazebo stage with a sweaty bottle of beer in his hand. Johnny Barr looked puzzled for a minute, but he clapped Junior's shoulder, shook his hand, and gave him the mike.

Junior said something to the band. He looked red-eyed and dazzled as he started singing "Why Have You Left the One You Left Me For?" There was whiskey in his voice, but he knew all the words and carried the tune pretty well.

"The fat sot can sing, cain't he?" Tack dragged on his cigarette.

Tres felt his face color. He had a claustrophobic sensation, as if the crowd were suffocating him. The bright lights hurt his eyes, and the laughter and the little kids with pink tufts of cotton candy stuck to their faces jangled his nerves.

Junior finished the song after what seemed to Tres a very long time. Someone in the crowd yelled, "Where's Johnny Barr?"

Tres wound his way across the concrete slab through the crowd. He stood in front of the gazebo and crooked his finger at Junior.

Junior looked surprised to see him and smiled broadly. He said, "Night, folks," and stumbled down the stairs.

Tres put his arm around Junior's waist and said, "Come on, Daddy."

"Where're we goin'?" Junior asked.

"I'll walk you to the café. I ain't seen it yet."

They walked in silence, away from the crowd. There was a fistfight in the parking lot. Ordinarily, Tres would have stopped to watch it, but he steered Junior toward Main Street. The storefronts were dark and empty looking, and a cold breeze blew down the black street. The wind seemed to sober Junior up some.

"Oh, me," Junior kept saying over and over.

Tres felt a sharp stab of anger. All the loneliness of the past week came back to him. He tried to tell himself that nothing so bad had happened at the dance, but he couldn't convince himself. Hadn't Junior moved away to keep from being a drunk?

The café was just outside town, on the highway. Tres kept Junior moving until they reached the Tip Top. Junior let them in, and for a moment they were awash in the funny flashing blue-and-green neon light, until Junior found the light switch.

"Why don't you take a shower while I heat up some coffee and look around?"

Junior nodded and went upstairs. It was the same café, but Junior had painted the walls white and put new red vinyl cushions in the booths and on the counter stools. He'd done a lot of work for just one week. It looked clean and true to the sign in the window that said OPEN FOR BUSINESS—MONDAY 7:00 A.M. Tres found a pot full of coffee and plugged it in.

By the time the coffee was hot, Junior was sitting at the counter, the heels of his boots hooked over a rung of his stool. He had a hangdog look on his face as he slugged back the coffee.

"The place looks great, Daddy. You done a lot of hard work."

Junior shook his head slowly. "I don't know. I was fine till this afternoon. I never done anything on my own."

Junior looked over Tres's head to the front door. "I

got this picture in my mind. Here it is: Monday morning comes. I got my apron on, this big grin on my face, and no one comes. No one at all."

"That ain't gonna happen, Daddy."

"Every time I think on it, every hair on my head stands up, and it feels like my blood turns to ice. My teeth is goin' to start chatterin' next."

Tres told himself over and over, Don't say it, don't say, don't—"Listen, Daddy. You can always come home. I sure miss you."

"Don't think I ain't tempted."

"Trouble is, you'd never leave again." Tres felt the truth, like a smack in the face, hit him at last. "And then you'd never know. You'd always wonder if you would have been happier, and you'd hate me and Granddaddy."

"You're all right without me?"

"It's real weird, but I reckon I'll get used to it. I've been reading that Betty Crocker cookbook, and I learned how to use the washing machine."

They grinned at each other. Tres had forgotten how easy it was to be with Junior.

"I'm sorry I cut the fool tonight," Junior said. "I've been lonesome and scared."

"Daddy, I think this here situation is like ropin'. I take a deep breath and see myself makin' a good throw every time. If I choke, I can't do it, I just can't. But if I tell myself, 'Tres Bomer, you're the best,' then it all comes together for me."

There was a loud honk in the parking lot. Tres opened

the door, to see Coot and Tack waiting for him in Tack's red convertible.

"I'll try to remember what you said," Junior said.

"I'll be by on Monday. I bet I'll have to stand in line to get in," Tres said, walking backward to the car.

Tres got in beside Coot. He hoped they'd see that he didn't want to talk and let him alone.

"You look like your brain has shorted out." Tack pulled onto the highway.

"Long day," Tres muttered.

"Don't worry none about your girl." Tack smiled. "I took care of her for you."

"Give it a break, Tack," Coot said nervously.

"It was easy, Tres. Don't make a hero out of me," Tack continued.

They sped down the highway. Dark canyon walls rose up on either side.

" 'Fore the night was over, she told me I was a baa lamb," Tack said.

"A *baa* lamb?" Tres asked. What was that?

"Cow flop, Tack," Coot hooted. "Only person ever called you that was Mama."

Tres felt a stirring of resentment deep inside himself. A lot of times with Tack he felt as if a herd of bulls had been kicking him in the teeth.

"Funny you should say that about the baa lamb," Tres said. He hadn't planned it. It just came out.

"Why?" asked Tack.

"Well, she told me your breath smelled. Said it wasn't

human—through-the-roof bad was how she described it."

"She never." Tack looked smug.

"Bad enough to make you puke. Those were her exact words."

"Shut up, you little runt, or I'll pull over and beat your face in." Tack accelerated, causing the car to shudder in the wind.

Tres looked at Tack's big hand on the wheel. It was square-looking, with knotted veins on the surface. He couldn't help himself. "Yeah," he added. "She said the only reason you danced with someone her age was the girls your age already knew about your sheep—oh, yeah—*baa lamb* breath."

"Are you crazy, Bomer?" Coot hissed.

They shot past a cove of trees, and Tack swerved to the side of the highway, jamming the brake pedal hard. The rear end broke to the left and the convertible spun halfway around before it came to a sudden halt.

Tres felt himself go cold. Boy oh boy oh boy, he thought. I'm really going to get it now.

Tack threw the door open on his side. He came toward Tres on the passenger side, but froze suddenly in his tracks.

Tres and Coot turned around, to see the flashing red gumdrop on the highway patrol car.

"Bad news," Coot said. Tres didn't think so.

"Problem with another critter?" the highway patrolman said as he climbed out of his car.

Tack stood stock-still for a minute. "No, sir. My little brother's sick. Bad stomachache from the fair. I was tryin' to get him home fast, but I feared he was goin' to get sick all over the car."

The patrolman shone his flashlight in Coot's face. It looked white as a stone. "That so, son?"

Coot nodded.

"You boys have a lot of trouble, seems like. I'm going to follow you home. Give you an escort, like," the patrolman said.

"I'll walk on home," Tres said. He got out of the car. "Just live up the way."

Tres felt his legs shake as he watched the cars pull onto the highway. He walked down the road in the dark, grinning slightly. I'm the Red Baron, Tack, he thought. Shot you down this time.

But something nagged at him after a few minutes. A tiny voice in his brain said, "But, Tres, your horse is in the hands of a reckless, mean-tempered fool. And a fool that ain't got no scruples, either."

THE next morning, Tres woke with the sure feeling that the heifer had had her calf. He pulled on some jeans and ran outside, to find her, still round as a watermelon, calmly eating hay.

"A watched pot don't boil," Senior said. "You take her out to the pasture again. Let her be with the rest of the herd."

Tres was beginning to agree. By late afternoon, when it was time to check the herd, he led her behind Sissy Belle to Slaughter Creek. He let Sissy Belle find the spot where she wanted to cross the creek, and he marveled that she splashed through without any shenanigans.

The heifer still limped, but all the swelling was gone. There was an ugly place on her foot, where Tres was afraid she might lose a core of dead tissue, but otherwise she was fine.

As the heifer took off into the brush, Tres prayed she wouldn't break a leg or be attacked by hungry coyotes or develop lump jaw or wander too far off or die. If everything went predictably, Tres knew that the list of hazards was endless.

By the time he'd checked the herd, the sun was down low and the trees along the creekbed looked dark. Sissy Belle clopped along, snorting and puffing. Tres felt lonesome, the way he had every evening since Junior had moved to town.

Worrying about Junior and the heifer had put Robin out of Tres's mind for a while. He wondered if she was mad at him for leaving in a hurry the night before, or if she understood. He wondered if she'd ever let him kiss her again. He ran events through his head in slow motion and felt as if he were right back at the dance, kissing Robin under the tree.

A deer shot out of the brush and jumped over a bush in front of them. Sissy Belle jerked her head, laid her ears back, and bucked Tres out of the saddle. He hit the ground hard and slid through a wet cow splat. The breath was knocked out of him, and as he sat up, his head was swimming around and around.

When he could stand, Sissy Belle was just a speck in

the distance, bucking and snorting her way home. The front of his shirt and pants was smeared with stinking manure.

"I'm glad this happened!" Tres screamed at her retreating form. "I'd almost forgotten how much I hate you!"

By the time he'd crossed the creek and could see the lights of the ranch house in the distance, Tres was shaking mad and making vows to himself.

"I solemnly swear I ain't ever goin' to have a no-'count mount again as long as I live, that's number one. Number two, I'm goin' to sell that mule to a paste factory as soon as I get Mariah, so's I never have to lay eyes on her again."

ten

res woke up Monday morning feeling nervous and jittery. He didn't calm down until the school bus passed the Tip Top and he saw plenty of cars and pickups parked in front.

This time last week he was so mad at Junior that he didn't even feel like seeing him. Now he was pulling for him to make a go of it at the Tip Top.

He wanted to talk to Robin and explain about Friday night, but she never rode the bus in the mornings, and she wasn't on it Monday afternoon. He'd planned to get off the bus at the café and visit with Junior, but low clouds, wet and stormy looking, moved in from the north. If rain was on the way, he needed to check the heifer before it set in.

By the time the bus let him off at Slaughter Creek, the sky was so dark that the oncoming cars sped by with their headlights on. A cold wind whipped his hat off, and he had to chase it down the road.

His granddaddy and Juarez weren't around, so he ate some beef jerky and drank a glass of milk. When he walked out on the back porch, he had an edgy feeling. Something dangerous was building. He ran across the pasture and climbed the windmill to the platform. To the northwest he saw a thin blue streak on the horizon, just below the storm clouds.

His granddaddy always called them blue whistlers, but to everyone else they were blue northers. They came down suddenly from the north, and their passing could be dry and clear or full of freezing rain and snow.

Tres remembered one that came through when he was a little kid. Some of Senior's best cattle suffocated because their nostrils froze and they couldn't breathe through their mouths. Others wallowed in the snowdrifts without feed. Tres would never forget the big old heifers, dead and bloated, being hauled off in trucks after the storm.

After that, Junior built sheds in the pastures for a windbreak, and Senior bought a green tractor to move hay to the herd. But a heifer pregnant with her first calf might not fare too well.

He climbed down and ran back to the house. His granddaddy and Juarez were standing in the kitchen, hunched over the radio.

"Greetings from the Arctic!" the weatherman said. "A strong Arctic front with a layer of moisture over five thousand feet is racing toward the Panhandle. Strong winds and heavy snowfall—"

The rest of the report was cut off as Senior barked orders.

"Juarez, you and Tres get those bales of hay ready to move. If it freezes, those heifers will starve without plenty of hay."

They pulled on down jackets, heavy socks, and leather gloves. Tres and Juarez stacked giant round bales of hay by the barn door. Tres could feel the temperature steadily dropping. By dusk, icy blasts of wind were followed by a powdery snow that fell so rapidly it blanketed the pastures as far as he could see.

He wanted to get to his heifer, make sure she was all right. He wanted to bring her back to the barn, where nothing could happen to her, but there was the whole herd to consider. If he left now, before the work was done, Granddaddy would never forgive him.

The RC Cola thermometer registered six degrees when he climbed into the cab of the John Deere next to Juarez. They began to move the hay slowly across the pastures.

The tractor lights cast queer yellow streaks on the white ground. Soon the falling snow limited his vision to about twenty feet. They finally spotted part of the herd, their tails tucked and their heads low against the wind. They were clustered together against one of the sheds.

Tres opened the cab door and felt as if someone had pelted him with freezing buckshot. The cows bawled as he searched among them for his heifer. His heart fell when he couldn't find her.

They went back for more hay, and again the tractor rumbled across the pasture, to a shed in an upper northwest pasture. The rest of the herd was bunched up at the windbreak, lowing. He knew that by morning they'd want water and go to the creek, even if it was frozen over.

Juarez seemed to understand that Tres had to look for his heifer. When he didn't find her at the second shed, he had to fight down panic. She'd moved off from the herd, and that could mean only one thing in this kind of weather—she was calving.

Tres thought about his options. If he left her out all night, she and the calf could die. If he went after her, there was no guarantee he'd find her in this storm, especially now that dark had set in. And what shenanigans would Sissy Belle pull in a blizzard? He swallowed hard to keep back the tears.

Juarez drove the tractor into the barn and went up to the house. Tres went to the stable and saddled Sissy Belle. She snorted her complaints as he pulled on a wool cap with a bill and earflaps to keep his ears from getting frostbitten. He tied on a pair of leather chaps to make his legs warmer and swung into the saddle.

"Where do you think you're goin'?" His granddaddy stood inside the barn door, looking for all the world like Superman with gray hair and wrinkles.

"I ain't leavin' her out there in the weather, Granddaddy." He told Senior about not being able to find the heifer at the sheds.

"She's probably in a stand of trees. That calf she's

having is half longhorn. It's got a chance to make it."

"I ain't takin' that chance, Granddaddy. She's halter broken. If I can find her, I can lead her back."

"We just heard the weather report. The windchill factor should fall to forty below tonight. That dang mule could dump you in the snow," Senior said.

"I'm goin', anyways," Tres said.

"Look here, boy. You've done your part of the bargain. You've suffered this mule and gotten the heifer to calve. This here storm was rotten luck. I've got some money put back. If the heifer and her calf don't make it, I'll buy that horse you want."

Senior never pleaded with anyone for anything, but Tres could hear it in his voice, and it touched him.

"It ain't just the horse anymore. I've been takin' care of that heifer so long now I don't know how to stop. I can't leave her out in the middle of a blue norther, her ready to drop her first calf," Tres said.

Senior just shook his head. Tres knew that he wanted to forbid him to go, but he would never forbid an action he secretly respected.

"Besides, Sissy Belle probably won't make it more than a mile, anyways," Tres continued, and grinned.

Sissy Belle trotted out the stable door, and soon Senior was just a speck in the yellow rectangle of light.

The wind blowing off the snow cuffed and slapped at them, but Tres felt better. He'd made a decision, and there was nothing more to do but find the heifer. Even Sissy Belle seemed invigorated by the freezing weather and picked up her pace.

There was an eerie light darkness over the snow-covered pastures, but the snow fell so hard that he could see only a few feet in front of him. Turning Sissy Belle, he took a shortcut through the trees. He checked the fencelines by the sheds and roamed through the herd again, looking for the heifer.

The herd had banded together in groups, their warm breath a cloud of steam rising like campfire smoke over an Indian village.

When Tres moved away from the second shed, the howling winds blew snow that stung his face and hung on his eyelashes. He was so bone cold that he felt shaky.

He decided to check a pasture farther north that had a stand of mesquite trees. The heifer had strayed up there in the past, and it was the only place left to look. They followed the fenceline a couple of miles until Tres reluctantly turned Sissy Belle toward the trees. He hated to leave the fenceline, because the countryside looked unfamiliar blanketed in white.

They seemed to have ridden so far that he was sure they'd missed the trees, but finally the mesquite thicket loomed ahead. The trees looked transformed under their white burdens.

Tres's heart accelerated. If she wasn't here, he'd have to go back without her, maybe find her frozen stiff in the morning. He shook his head and shuddered. Unthinkable.

He wound through the thicket, listening for sounds, but the howling wind was the only noise he could hear. He got down from the saddle and walked in front of

Sissy Belle. He wanted to move around some and see if he could spot tracks, but the deep new snow and the frost hanging in the air made it hard to make out anything, until he saw the blood track.

Tres felt the skin prickle on the back of his neck. He walked faster through the snow, pulling Sissy Belle and making her stumble. Tres saw the calf first, a wobbly little bull calf. He looked like all longhorn calves, with his big ears and funny long legs. Standing beside his mother in the snow, he reminded Tres of a jackrabbit.

As Tres approached, the heifer struggled to her feet. She looked all right, but she seemed weak and shaky.

He tried to talk to her as he fastened the halter on her, but his teeth chattered. He picked up the new calf and climbed awkwardly into the saddle with it. He held it tightly, but his arms were so numb that he could barely feel anything.

Sissy Belle trotted out of the trees toward the middle of a ravine.

"Stupid mule!" Tres yelled. He had to get back to the fenceline and follow it to the lower pastures.

The snow had made the heifer sore-footed, and she didn't seem to want to move. She struggled at the end of the rope, and for a time they all seemed at odds. Finally, he managed to get Sissy Belle moving where he wanted her to go, and the heifer plodded after.

Tres's eyes burned in the swooping winds. He blinked again and again, trying to spot the fenceline. Sissy Belle jerked at the reins, trying to turn, and almost made him drop the calf in the snow.

"This ain't the time for one of your fits." He regained his balance and turned her toward the fenceline again.

The blowing snow stung his face and eyes. He tried to pull his kerchief up over his nose, but the wind blew it away. Over and over he thought he saw the fenceline, but it was all inside his head—what he wished he could see.

He finally stopped and looked around. Only a few feet in front of him and a few feet behind him were visible. What he could see looked completely different in the swirling snow. He felt a rising fear. They should have hit the fenceline at least a mile back.

He tried to sort out his sense of direction, but the more he looked, the more confused he got.

I've been over every foot of this ranch hundreds of times. How can I be lost? The thought was unbelievable to him. Snatches of half-forgotten Sunday-school prayers came back to him.

A pack of coyotes howled off to his left. It was the loneliest sound he'd ever heard. When he glanced back at the heifer, she appeared ready to drop. The baby calf was humped up and looked as if it were trying to die, and he himself was feeling numb and completely exhausted.

Tres didn't care about the quarter horse anymore. If he could just see the lights of the ranch and get them all home, he'd gladly give the horse up.

eleven

Sissy Belle brayed loudly and started off without Tres's permission. He tried to rein her in, but she seemed determined to go. He finally decided it was better to keep moving than to stay there and freeze to death.

There was no way to know how much time had passed. The only noises in the white wilderness were the howling wind and the coyotes. He gave up looking for landmarks and pulled his jacket around his face.

Tres wanted to sleep and thought for a time he was in his bed, warm and cozy. A voice loomed over the bed and said, "You *wake* up, and I mean *right this minute*, or you'll be frozen so stiff we'll be using you for a poker all winter."

Thinking it was Senior, he opened his eyes and realized that he was still in the saddle with the baby calf. He decided he must be talking to himself and determined to stay awake after that. He'd heard about hypothermia and how people caught in snowstorms sometimes suddenly felt warm and went to sleep and never woke up.

"Hypothermia, hypothermia," he whispered. It sounded like something you'd put coffee or lemonade in.

"That's a thermos, stupid," he muttered to himself.

He watched Sissy Belle's ears flop back and forth, but the cold wind stung his eyes. He tried to count backward from a hundred. He was about to drop off to sleep again, when he looked up and saw lights in the distance. Sissy Belle squealed, and Tres's heart did a hitch when he made out Junior standing in the road.

He was never sure what happened next. He remembered Junior tucking him in bed late that night as if he were a little kid and telling him they had been about to call a search party together.

"I'm glad you had a lot of customers this morning, but I sure am glad you came out tonight," Tres said. "Are you and Granddaddy talkin' again?"

"Sort of. By the way, I remember something good Miz Gertrude told me about Sissy Belle."

"What's that?" Tres asked.

"No matter where she is, she can always find her way home."

"She sure saved us. I was some lost out there. She kept wanting to head home, but I didn't know what she was doing. That was the worst scared I've ever been." Tres turned up the dial on the electric blanket.

"Well, you keep that heifer and her little calf in the barn. I have a feelin' your granddaddy will have 'em sold when the weather fairs up." Junior ruffled his hair.

Tres shut his eyes tight. His feelings were like a hopelessly tangled rope. Somehow, Junior's leaving was all snarled up with Sissy Belle's coming and the way he'd sold her short. Twisted in with all that was the struggle he'd been through to keep the heifer alive. It all raveled back to the quarter horse, any way you looked at it.

"What's wrong?" Junior asked.

"If wanting that horse so much has brought all this trouble, what's having her going to be like?"

"It'll be great!" Junior's eyes shone.

"I was about to decide she was bad luck," Tres muttered.

"Don't be a knucklehead. You ain't the kind of person that depends on good luck or bad luck. You make your own luck."

Tres didn't say anything. He wanted Junior to keep talking.

"You get what you want 'cause you don't give up. I aim to become more that way myself," Junior said.

"I sort of promised myself I'd give the horse up if we got home safe, but I don't feel like it no more. Maybe I lack backbone," Tres said.

"Promises made in the blowin' snow don't count. That's the eleventh commandment, to my way of thinkin'." The look on Junior's face was so serious that Tres started laughing.

THE wind died down in the night, and the snow stopped falling early in the morning. It didn't melt off until the end of the week, when the sun came back out. Senior told him that it was one of the worst blue northers on record, but the herd made it through, with only a couple of losses.

Tres had a high fever and a sore throat that developed into a hacking cough. He spent the week in bed, sleeping and feeling dizzy. Junior went back to the café, leaving him in the hands of Senior and Juarez. Tres didn't think either one of them was cut out to nurse human beings. He was grateful for the soup and pudding that Junior brought over every afternoon.

Friday morning, he woke late with a dull headache. He heard a commotion outside and looked out the window to see a cattle truck roll up to the barn.

Juarez led the heifer and her calf to the truck, and Senior pulled Sissy Belle behind.

"Oh, Lord," Tres said. He pulled on a pair of jeans and ran out the back door to the barn.

"Just what in the pluperfect hell are you doin' out here sick without any clothes on?" Senior thundered at him.

Tres looked down and realized he had forgotten his boots and he didn't have a shirt on.

"What's happening here, Granddaddy?"

"This here's Mr. Safire, and he's goin' to take these animals off our hands and give us good money for 'em," Senior said.

111

Tres reached out and shook Mr. Safire's hand. He didn't look any too pleased to be shaking the hand of a sick person.

"He ain't takin' Sissy Belle, too, is he?" Tres asked. His heart was in his throat.

"He's kindly agreed to take her off our hands, yes," Senior answered.

"Well, he can't, Granddaddy. I mean—"

Senior cut him off. "Now look-a-here, Mr. Smart Aleck. Your daddy ain't here to look after her no more, and he was the one what brung her out here in the first place. She's served her purpose for you now. You're gettin' that fancy horse next week, and you won't be needin' her."

Tres looked at Sissy Belle and felt a sudden rush of love. Oh, sure, he'd hated her and cussed her, and she'd embarrassed him at different times. He'd had moments when he was glad there wasn't a gun in his hand, because he probably would have shot her. But the fact was, she'd saved his life and made it possible for his best dream to come true. They'd been through things in the last few weeks that no one else in the world would ever really know of.

"Truth is, Granddaddy, I will be needin' her. See, those fence posts over yonder need to be hauled up to the pasture, and I figure she's strong enough to lug them." Tres's speech sent him into a coughing spell.

Senior scratched his jaw and looked as if he were figuring out where his advantage lay.

"If she can't haul, then what? I ain't havin' no pet

mule around here to feed." Senior scowled and hooked his thumbs in the band at the top of his chaps.

The scene had made Mr. Safire red in the face, and he busied himself loading the heifer and the calf on the truck. Juarez looked thoroughly bored and spat.

Tres racked his brain. "I like her, that's what, and I'll find a way to make her useful. If ever I don't, Mr. Safire can have her," he said at last.

"If this don't beat all." Senior let his breath out and pushed his mashed-up Stetson down on his head.

"You couldn't wait to get shut of her . . . this man's willing to pay good money . . . now out of a clear blue sky . . ." He stopped and got a look on his face that said he was surrounded by a bunch of idiots he'd never understand.

Tres had seen that look before. He held his breath.

"All right, all right! Juarez, gee that mule around and put her in the stable. Tres, it's a blue-eyed wonder you ain't caught the pneumonia. Get yourself back to bed, and I mean right this minute!"

Tres was so relieved he felt weak in the knees. He'd been afraid to ask what Mr. Safire's plans were for Sissy Belle, but he couldn't imagine they'd be pleasant.

He was sorry later that he never got to say good-bye to the heifer, but how do you *do* that, anyways? he asked himself.

Sunday afternoon was warm and sunny. The grass had thawed out and was yellow, streaked with new green shoots.

Juarez hitched the horse trailer to the pickup, and Tres and Senior went to the Taylors' to give Tack his money and bring Mariah home. Tres was sure it was the proudest day of his life.

He was glad the Taylors weren't home and he could hand Tack the money and leave without having to visit. He couldn't wait to ride her.

After he took her across Slaughter Creek and back, Senior wanted to ride her. When Juarez climbed on to take a turn, Tres slipped into the kitchen and called Robin.

"Where have you been all week?" she asked.

"Sick. But I'm okay now. Listen, I've got something to show you. If you'll meet me down the road halfway, you could come over for a while," Tres said.

"What is it? Give me a hint," she said.

"Well, let's just say it could change your mind about cowboys forever," Tres said.

"Oh, I did that a long time ago," she said.

"Really?" he asked.

"Really. But I'm always open to more evidence. Meet you in thirty minutes," she said, and hung up.

He started down the road on Mariah. A little longhorn calf peered through the barbed wire at them. Tres fingered the rope at his side, but decided against roping the calf for now.

"Plenty of time for you later," he said to the calf. "I've got an important appointment."

DONA SCHENKER is a former librarian and author of more than twenty published stories for young readers. A Texas native, she lives with her husband and two sons in San Antonio. *Throw a Hungry Loop* is her first novel.